Mojave Showdown

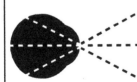

This Large Print Book carries the
Seal of Approval of N.A.V.H.

A NED CODY NOVEL

Mojave Showdown

L. J. Martin

THORNDIKE PRESS
A part of Gale, a Cengage Company

Farmington Hills, Mich • San Francisco • New York • Waterville, Maine
Meriden, Conn • Mason, Ohio • Chicago

**LIBRARY OF CONGRESS CIP DATA ON FILE.
CATALOGUING IN PUBLICATION FOR THIS BOOK
IS AVAILABLE FROM THE LIBRARY OF CONGRESS**

ISBN-13: 978-1-4328-5649-6 (hardcover)

Published in 2018 by arrangement with Viking, an imprint of Penguin
Publishing Group, a division of Penguin Random House LLC

Printed in Mexico
1 2 3 4 5 6 7 22 21 20 19 18

MOJAVE SHOWDOWN

CHAPTER ONE

He watched with cold, dark, unflinching eyes.

Patience was the first thing the desert taught him and he'd learned well. He'd knelt, unmoving, in the same spot, while the sun crossed a quarter of the morning sky and the roses and golds of the morning turned to watery grays and washed out, wavering tans.

Mangas Saragosa crouched in an outcropping of dried blood-red volcanic rock, and eyed the wagons below. His broad muscular back gleamed with sweat in the noonday sun. His long black hair, tattooed torso and legs blended with the shadows of the mesquite which fought for root-hold in the basalt behind him. Unmoving, Saragosa knew he could not be seen. He was never seen, if he did not wish it.

Saragosa kept his rifle well below the rocks to prevent the brass receiver of his Henry from catching and reflecting the sun's powerful rays. Carefully, almost reverently, he reached into the leather pouch that hung from a rawhide thong around his neck pulled out a bud of peyote, and began chewing it slowly.

The first team of stock and wagons crested the rise known to the white eyes as Windy Gap, and reined up, awaiting the second.

True to its name, the wind whistled and curled through the gap, and the dust rose in turbulent vortexes. A raven, cawing wildly as he tried to catch an updraft was buffeted one way and then the other. The bird sassed the Indian in the rocks below, but the white men paid no heed.

Behind the lead rig, Jud McGrath, a long line skinner, perched on the wagon seat eight feet above the deep-rutted road. He spoke in a low encouraging tone to the span of eighteen hundred pound wheel horses directly in front of the wagon as they leaned into their collars. In front of them the pointers — most intelligent of the mules — strained against their own collars. Ahead of them pulled the sixes, then the eights, and so forth up to the lead span, the twenties.

Behind the massive wagon upon which Jud was riding trailed another equally large wagon attached to the first. A smaller wagon with a five hundred gallon iron water tank mounted on it brought up the rear. Water was a must. The stock would never survive the fifty miles between water holes on the Death Valley-Mojave road without it.

Eighteen head of mules and two horses strained against forty-five thousand pounds of wagons, water, and borax. Jud was one of the few men in the West qualified to handle such a team. He had come to the desert in search of silver and gold and, like most men who'd made the journey, found sweat and hard work instead.

He was careful not to touch any of the metal on the wagon. To do so would have resulted in a badly blistered hand. But this was the last trip of the season. From the middle of June to the middle of September the skinners and swampers would be mending tack and corrals. It was just too damned hot to make the long runs during that time. Only lizards and snakes braved the desert then and even they only came out a night. Jud hated mending tack. This trip was the end for him. He had decided to go home. He hadn't seen his family in Arkansas since he'd left in '72, eight years earlier. Neither he nor his family could read or write, so he hadn't heard a word from them in all that time. Perhaps they'd gone on to meet their

Maker, but Jud figured the trip was worth the chance. He had a poke full of earnings, and in three days, when they reached Mojave, he would leave on the westbound train for Bakersfield. Then another would take him north to Sacramento, then a third east. The southern connection of the railroad was still on the drawing boards.

Ahead of Jud and his swamper, Dallas Trumbell, loomed the crest of Windy Gap and the toughest of the turns on the ten day trip. By the time they were full into the turn, the lead mules would be straining against their collars across a ravine opposite from the wagons and twelve feet above. Negotiating the turn without dragging the wagons off the road and tumbling into the gorge meant the team had to pull against itself. While the five lead spans made the gee — or right turn — the back four spans would have to pull to the haw, or left. Four of the mules on the rear spans would have to jump the chain to accomplish this, and their spans would pull at a forty-five degree angle, fighting to keep the wagons on the road.

As the lead span went into the turn, Jud yelled an echoing "Whoaaaa."

Dallas Trumbell, the swamper, dismounted from the lead near left side mule and worked his way back to the tens. He touched the underbelly of the near mule and the animal jumped the chain. He did the same to the eights, then the sixes. The pointer mare was already across the chain, a three foot jump, by the time he reached her. "Good mule, Betsy," he said, praising her.

He walked on past where Jud perched high above, and checked the first five-foot high front wheel of the wagon, then the seven-foot rear wheel. He carefully went from wheel hub to wheel hub feeling for excess heat until he had checked all twelve. As he bent down, he removed his skinning knife from a scabbard at his belt, then ran the blade under the inch thick, twelve-inch iron tire to see how far it had pulled away from its wooden rim.

"Won't be long before we'll be havin' to leave this 'un with the wheelwright," he grumbled. It was no easy task removing the wheel, much less tightening the thousand pound iron tire. "Let's give her a go," the small, wiry swamper said as he passed by Jud who then climbed down from his lofty seat.

Dallas worked his way to the lead mules while Jud took his position in the saddle of the near wheel horse. The padded saddle gave him more control over the critical path of the wheel horses, and the pointers responded quicker knowing they were within whip range.

As Dallas reached the twenties, Jud cracked the whip. Its rifle-shot snap and his loud "Git up" echoed down Windy Gap. Again and again the whip cracked. The bells on the mule's necks rang in cadence as they plodded forward, then intermittently as the rear of the team fought to keep the wagons on the road.

Negotiating the climb and turn, they reached the straight behind the lead rig. Jud yelled, "Whoaaa," and the mules halted. He regained his wagon seat and Dallas walked the hundred feet back from the lead span. He stopped and cursed the near side sixes mule who had not yet recrossed the chain as the others had. Finally getting the animal to cross over, Dallas deftly climbed up and seated himself beside Jud.

Pulling his wide-brimmed hat off, Dallas mopped his brow, smearing the rivulets of dust-covered sweat across his forehead. "That was smooth as Frenchy's watered-down whiskey," Dallas said smiling. He spat a long stream of tobacco juice into the dust far below.

Jud reached under the seat and removed a canvas-covered tin canteen. He unstoppered it and took a long pull, then handed it to his swamper. "We get any better at this and Delemeter's liable to give us an extra wagon and ten more mules to tote it."

Dallas laughed, then suddenly turned serious. "You got enough in your poke to make your trip home? I got a little set aside if'n you need it."

Jud shook his head. "I got plenty, but I'm obliged for the offer. You've been a damn fine hand and a good friend, Dallas." A little embarrassed at his own sentimentality, Jud looked straight ahead as he spoke. "I'll be talkin' to Delemeter a'fore I catch that train. If'n I have anything to say about it, he'll be givin' you this seat come September."

Before Dallas could express his thanks, his head caved in like a watermelon kicked with a pointed boot. He somersaulted sideways out of the high seat. Jud heard the report of the rifle as Dallas went over the set's low rail to sprawl in the dust.

Jud looked up for the source of the cracking shot, then thought a bolt of lightning must have struck him, its white heat piercing his skull. By the time he lay in the dust beside his friend, his thinking had ended forever. His lifeblood slowly soaked into the desert, mingling with that of his swamper.

Horace Trumbell, Dallas Trumbell's

cousin, had been standing on the seat of the lead rig waving to Jud and Dallas when the rifle shot rang out from the rocks. The second shot had come even before he had time to move. Thad Spencer, the long line skinner who sat beside him, dragged him back down into the seat.

"What the hell, Horace!" Thad shouted, crouching behind the high back seat. "What the hell happened?"

"Somebody done shot Jud and Dallas," Horace said, jumping down from the seat to the roadbed on the far side from the rocks. Thad leaped down behind him, almost landing on the smaller man. They peered through the four inch thick spokes of the wheels, searching for the hidden marksman.

A tall tattooed Indian stood facing their wagon. He raised his rifle high, his high-pitched scream reverberating through Windy Gap, mingling with the wind. Then suddenly he was gone. Both men squinted in surprise.

Horace turned to the skinner. "Did he leave? Do you think I ought to go see if they're alive?"

"What do you think he wants?" Thad asked. "I never heard of nobody stealing borax."

14

"I ain't heered of no Indian trouble 'round here in more'n ten years," Horace said in a loud whisper. "It must be the stock. And if he wants 'em, I say given 'em to him. I got no urge to get my hide ventilated over a bunch of knot-headed, hell-on-the-hoof mules."

"Maybe we could cut the twenties loose and ride the hell out of here," Thad offered breathlessly.

"The way that ol' boy shoots, we wouldn't get ten feet." Realizing that whispering was ridiculous, Horace raised his voice to a normal tone. "I bet he wants the stock, and I bet he only wants one team, otherwise he'd a' shot us down just like Jud and Dallas. I'm a' gonna go on back there and cut 'em loose. An' I'll see if'n those boys is alive. We can't get both teams back no how."

"You think I ought to dig the Springfield out?" Thad asked, referring to the old rifle buried under the wagon seat.

"It would probably blow up in your face. You never shot it?" Horace asked.

"Can't say as I have. And I'm no gunfighter."

"Let's leave it be," Horace advised. "We'd be dead by now if that Indian wanted us that way. I'm gonna step out there with my hands in the air, an' if'n I don't get shot,

I'm gonna cut that stock loose."

Catching sight of a plum-colored dress and parasol he recognized, Ned Cody crossed Chester Avenue, dodging one of the town's new-fangled horse drawn street cars as it barreled down the thoroughfare. He pulled up short, bracketed by two wavering bicycles, their front wheels three times the size of their rear. He shook his head, disgusted that full grown men would take to mechanical contraptions rather than stick with fine horseflesh. Continuing, he wove his way through a cadre of Chinese laborers and between a group of mounted *vaqueros,* whose silver-studded tack glittered in the bright afternoon sun. "Place is getting too dang crowded." Cody mumbled grumpily as he stepped up onto the boardwalk.

He tipped his broad-brimmed felt hat to several townspeople as he strolled along behind the girl just ahead of him. She'd raised the parasol just high enough so Cody could make out a mass of honey blond hair falling to below her shoulders. When she stopped to read an advertisement in the window of the dry goods store, he slipped quietly up behind her. The pamphlet was advertising a suffragette meeting to be held in the town hall the coming weekend.

"I suppose you'll be wantin' to wear pants next?" he teased, leaning his lanky frame against the green metal shutter at the window sill.

"Ned Cody! Don't you ever sneak up on a lady like that!" The girl's tone was brusque but her blue eyes sparkled. Ned took her hand in his and smiled down at her.

"Which way are you headin', Miss Nelson? Maybe a fella' could walk along with you a while. If you're headin' toward the courthouse, that is."

"It just so happens I am," Mary Beth Nelson said smiling. "But you best be keeping your hand-holding to the front porch. Neither my father, nor your voters, would approve."

When they'd reached the middle of the block, Ned suddenly turned into an alley. Mary Beth stopped, determined not to follow, but he tugged her in just out of sight of the street. Pulling her close with one hand as he pushed back his broad-brimmed hat with the other, Cody kissed her roughly. She clung to him a moment then pushed him away.

"Ned Cody, you are a scandal!"

Cody grinned. "If a fellow can't steal a kiss from his betrothed, then where's he to get one?"

"A fellow doesn't need a kiss until he's married," Mary Beth insisted, returning to the boardwalk. "Are you coming to dinner tonight, Sheriff Cody?" she asked, abruptly changing the subject.

"No ma'am, but I'll be along afterward to sit on the porch and steal another kiss."

She tossed a smile over her shoulder and started walking back the way they'd come. "We'll see about that," she said mischievously.

Ned watched her go, then turned and strode on down the street in the opposite direction. Crossing Eighteenth, he saw a familiar profile entering Callahan's Chop and Oyster House. He turned and with long strides hurried down the side street after him.

Banging through the swinging doors, Ned crossed the peanut and egg shell littered floor, and sidled up to the bar between two men. The man to his left, a Californio, was tall and lean, built somewhat like Cody himself. The other was massive, a half-head taller than Cody and as deep as he was broad. The Spaniard's features were straight and finely honed while those of the bigger man's were rounded and his hair thinning.

"I guess Bakersfield must be one of the quietest towns in the state," Ned said, his tone controlled and officious. "County deputies got time to belly up to the bar in midday."

Jimmy Callahan slapped a towel on the bar directly in front of the sheriff. "These boys is here on official business, Ned. I needed some help figuring out if this new batch of beer is as good as the last."

"Well, *amigo,*" Alvarado Cuen, the Californio, said, "set him up. We'll see if it's three for three." Cuen was the first Californio lawman in this part of the state. He slapped a nickel on the bar, then took a deep draw on his own mug, wiping the foam from his mustache with the back of his hand.

Jimmy drew another mug and slid it down the bar toward Theo Ratzlaff, the county's biggest deputy, who lifted his, letting Ned's slide by.

Ned took a deep draw on the mug, then reached under the bar, grabbed one of the bar towels that hung every six feet and wiped the foam from his mouth. "Why hell, Jimmy, that's green as a gourd. I want Al's nickel back."

Jimmy flipped the nickel into a cigar box on the back bar. "I'll buy yours, Cody. Al hasn't paid for his own yet."

"Jimmy," Cody asked, "how about whip-pin' up a little hang town fry while I have a meeting with the county's finest? You did get a fresh batch of oysters on the morning train?"

"Fresh as a new bride, Cody. You boys have a seat."

The saloon was beginning to fill up with drovers, drummers, *vaqueros,* clerks, all gathering at Callahan's for the noon meal. They all knew that Jimmy had the best food in town — as well as the prettiest saloon girls in California.

Cody, Ratzlaff, and Cuen took a round table along the wall underneath two bright-colored Bill Show posters. One featured Buffalo Bill's Wild West Show, the other, Pawnee Bill's.

Al Cuen pushed his black sombrero back off his head. It dangled behind him hanging from its rawhide tie. His dark eyes flashed as he surveyed the room. "Things have been strangely quiet, *amigo,*" he observed.

"It's too damn hot to get into trouble, Al," Ned replied. "Hell, nobody's got the gumption."

"Not how I see it, Ned." Theo Ratzlaff had been a lawman longer than either of the other two men and considered himself the true expert. "Heat always makes folks real crotchety. I'd be lookin' for a robbin' or a shootin' at anytime." Theo rubbed h is game shoulder as he talked. He'd taken a load of buckshot the year before and the shoulder still troubled him on occasion. "Sides', it's a full moon an' the boys will be really howlin' come Saturday night."

"Well, fellas, here's to peace and quiet," Ned announced, raising his mug and touching it to the others. "The last thing I want is to be chasin' some crotchety howler in this heat."

They drank up as Jimmy dropped a cast iron skillet in the middle of the table. One of the girls delivered three plates and forks.

The aroma of the eggs, bacon, oysters, and potatoes stole their attention, even away from the pretty bar girl, and as they spooned the mouth-watering concoction onto their plates, Jimmy returned to refill the mugs.

Before Theo Ratzlaff shoveled in the first forkful, he glanced up at Cody. "Mark my words," he cautioned, "this heat is trouble with a capital T."

Cody laughed. "Well Theo, I hope you're wrong. But if you're not, I hope it's high mountain trouble. I got a new split bamboo rod and I'd gladly dig a mess of worms if I had an excuse to get up to the high country. That's the kind of trouble I could stand about a week of."

"We should be so lucky," Theo mumbled, his mouth full of eggs and oysters.

CHAPTER TWO

The next morning, as prophesied by Theo, a telegram from Mojave hung pinned to Ned's office door.

A court hearing and a long explanation to Mary Beth as to why he had to handle the situation himself, rather than letting his deputies do it, detained Cody in Bakersfield an extra day. It was Mary Beth's dissatisfaction with Cody's job in the first place that had prevented them from setting a date. She seemed convinced that she could talk him into leaving the sheriff's office. But the stubborn lawman loved his job just slightly less than he loved the beautiful and persistent Miss Nelson.

He'd sent Al and Theo on ahead, with instructions to find out all they could about the crime, promising to meet them in Mojave the following day.

Early the next morning, Ned entered the train and took a window seat to best enjoy the slow, winding pull up into the Tehachapi Mountains.

The Southern Pacific lines, originating in both San Francisco and Sacramento, joined near Visalia in the middle of the San Joaquin Valley, then continued south through the valley's tules and swamps. The line passed between the majestic Sierra Nevada Mountains on the east and the Sierra Madres on the west. From Bakersfield, the line swung east, and climbed the Tehachapi Mountains to a town of the same name. A few miles beyond the mountain town, a flat expanse of desert spread out as far as the eye could see. At Mojave, the tracks branched, one line turned south heading for Los Angeles, while the other pointed almost due east. Another hundred miles through the wasteland, the Southern Pacific joined with the Atlantic and Pacific. It was planned that the two would follow the Mojave River. The planned line would leave the state, and cross into the Territory of Arizona at the Colorado River just below old Fort Mojave, to join the Atchison, Topeka & Santa Fe. The joining of the lines would tie the southern half of the United States together as the Union Pacific and Central Pacific had united the northern half back in 1869.

Tired of trying to decipher the smallish

type of the *Southern Californian* in the swaying train, Ned paused from his reading to watch the country roll by. It was convention time, and Grant was running for an unprecedented third term with Sherman trying to upset his bid. More and more, the name of an upstart from the House of Representatives, James Garfield, was being raised. Ned sighed, preferring the mountain scenery to the news of the Republican Convention.

The hills, now golden as the rains were well past, rose up on either side of the tracks. Scattered cattle and an occasional band of sheep grazed contentedly on the dry grass. The steep hills were spotted with green live oaks, gray-green scrub oaks, and hard shoulders of granite outcroppings. The blue-gray granite was highlighted with splotches of yellow and orange lichen. Red-tailed hawks circled lazily above.

The oaks became interspersed with digger pines as the train chugged past Keene. The bright sunlight was abruptly interrupted by the darkness of several short tunnels. Before Cody's eyes could become accustomed to the absence of light, the sun flared up again. The train leveled off into a high valley and slowed down as it reached Tehachapi — the last stop before the broad, foreboding expanse of the desert and the ramshackle town of Mojave.

Cody bought a soda water from a youngster who cooled them in a spring near the station. The boy had to run quickly from car to car since the train was only hesitating long enough to drop off and pick up mail, resupply the wood bin, and load one lone passenger. Then the train started up again, accelerating rapidly as it dropped out of the mountain valley, where oaks and pines were replaced with Joshua's sage, and a wide variety of cacti. The track into the desert was as straight as a beam of sunlight out of a hole in the clouds.

With every window wide open due to the heat, engine soot circulated freely throughout the cars. The hot, sooty wind evaporated the sweat that was rolling freely from Ned's pores. Cody dozed in the heat, only to be jerked awake as the train began slowing. It clanked and clattered and blew off steam in disgust, then settled in resignation to await its few boarding passengers at the Mojave station.

Big Jim Jackson stood impatiently on the board platform, searching for his boss. He smoothed down his full mutton-chop sideburns, then adjusted his thin-brimmed bowler hat. His sleeves were rolled up well past his elbows. A county deputy's badge was pinned to his wide, bright red suspenders rather than to his flannel shirt.

The conductor jumped down from the car door and dragged over a wooden box to be used as a step for departing passengers. The lanky man Big Jim awaited swung down easily behind the conductor. A .44 Dragoon Colt hung in a U.S. Cavalry holster at his side. It had been converted from cap and ball percussion to cartridge. Its wooden grips had been polished to a high glossy sheen.

Damn fool, Jackson thought. It had cost more to convert that old gun than it had to buy it new ten years before.

The sheriff tipped his hat to the conductor with his free hand, then extended the same hand to the waiting deputy. "Jackson," he said.

"Howdy, Sheriff." Big Jim grasped the rawboned hand. His greeting was friendly enough, but in his thoughts he pictured Cody climbing back onto the train and leaving Jackson to do his job — and run his town — as best he saw fit.

Cody carried a Visalia saddle and Spanish bridle and bit slung across his back. Jackson caught the odor of saddle soap as he eyed the young sheriff. He's as tall as I am, Jim thought, but he don't have any meat on

27

him. I could take him easy, faster'n a faro dealer can deal seconds. He ain't old enough to be smart. Just lucky.

The only thing about Cody that looked old enough for the sheriff's job, Jim thought, were his eyes. Deep brown, they creased with fine corner lines whenever Cody laughed or looked worried. They had a depth that seemed to have seen more than his years would warrant. Jackson had worked for Cody for a little over a year now, but being sixty-five miles from the county seat, they had seldom seen each other. That was fine with Big Jim. He liked to run his own show and this sheriff had some mighty strange ideas. Not like old Sheriff Howard. The deputies had made a lot more money working under Sheriff Howard.

Cody had been appointed sheriff after Howard had been murdered. Cody was young, seven years younger than Jackson in fact. It was too young in most folk's eyes. But he'd taken Johnny Tenkiller and the Urrea brothers in the same fight that had killed Sheriff Howard. That said a lot — but Jim chalked it off to luck, not skill.

Jackson was a county deputy and usually the only law to be found in the dusty town of Mojave. The town had flourished for a couple of years when it was the railhead, but now that the construction was finished, Mojave was little more than a freight way station for the many desert mines. Most of the saloons had already closed down, and most of the whores, gamblers and Chinese laborers had moved on to greener pastures.

Ned Cody dropped the saddle to the rough boards of the train platform, removed his hat and mopped his brow with a bright red kerchief. He pushed his wavy brown hair back under his broad-brimmed felt hat and fixed hard, gold-brown eyes on his deputy. "How much of a head start do you figure he has? Cody asked, skipping the formalities.

" 'Bout three days." Jackson answered. "He took the borax wagons about forty-five miles out of town. Yesterday, early afternoon. He killed the swamper on the second set of wagons with the first shot, then the driver. They was two teams travelin' together.

"Forty-five miles," Cody said thoughtfully. "That could be outside of Kern County. Not that it matters, I guess. What did he want with borax wagons?"

"Well, I don't mean he really took them," Jackson said, his tone a little condescending. "You ever seen a borax wagon?"

"No."

"Well, it's a sure bet he weren't after the

29

wagons or the borax. Those mules bring a thousand to two thousand a span."

"Why a span?" Ned asked.

"Two matching mules," Jackson explained, taking on a haughty schoolmaster's tone. "They train 'em together and keep 'em together. Anyways, with both the driver and Swamper shot, the other driver and swamper had no choice but to cut the stock loose. They waited awhile, hid out behind the wagon and as soon as they figured the shooter was gone, they cut the mules and wheel horses loose. Two men can't handle two of those teams. It takes a master skinner and swamper for each rig."

"Soon as they finished cuttin' 'em loose," Jackson continued, "the killer fired a few more shots, kickin' up gravel, and scattered the stock all to hell an' gone."

"Still no sign of any of the stock?" Cody asked.

Jackson shook his head. "Not a one showed up. He must have drove 'em off."

"A big job for one man," Cody said furrowing his brow. "How's everything else around this end of the county?"

As they talked, Ned strolled over to the livery car to collect his big roan from an attendant waiting at the head of a lowered ramp. The horse danced and kicked up his heels as he clattered down the fold-down door to the dirt, happy to be free of the confining railroad car.

Dropping his lead rope, saddle and bridle over a nearby rail, Ned walked around the roan. "You okay, Dancer," he whispered to the mount, scratching the white splash on the horse's forehead. Running his hands over Dancer's withers and long powerful legs, Ned carefully checked for injuries. He dug in a saddlebag for a curry, and after thoroughly combing the big horse's back, fitted a striped Mexican saddle blanket over it.

Jackson continued talking all the time Cody worked. "You know me, Ned," he said with assurance. "I got everything under control. Nobody gets out of line in my town. An' if they do, they wind up in my jail. Got three boys there now that thought they could hoorah the Silver Gunsight Saloon."

The night before, after receiving the telegram announcing that Cody was on his way, Jackson had rounded up three of the town's numerous drunks and stashed them behind bars. It always looked better if the jail was full.

Swinging the saddle into place, Ned freed the stirrup and cinch hooked to the horn and they fell into position of the far side of the gelding.

"Any marks on the stock that was stolen?" Ned asked, reaching under the belly of the roan, grasping the cinch and pulling it tight, after taking two turns through the cinch ring and back through the latigo.

"J.W.S. Perry," Jackson said, "the big boss of the Harmony Borax works, is over at the loadin' ramp. He and Delemeter, the head skinner, are waitin' for you. They can tell you anything else."

Cody bridled the roan while Jackson went off to fetch the gray he rode. While he waited, Cody led the roan in a circle — first to the left, then to the right — to make sure the saddle didn't bind the horse's flesh. A pinch of skin could land a man head first in the dirt. Finally satisfied, Ned mounted. Jackson returned and together they clopped out toward the borax terminal, a mile out of town, in silence. They reined up where two low dirt ramps had been constructed to raise the wagons to the level of the rail cars.

Ned dismounted and shook his head in amazement as he walked up the ramp alongside the massive borax wagon being offloaded by several Chinese coolies into a rail car. Ned inspected the wagon closely. He'd heard borax wagons carried over thirty-five tons. The rear wagon wheel was a foot taller than he himself was, and Ned topped six feet. Its iron tire was a foot wide and three quarters of an inch thick. The massive wooden wheel spokes were thicker than most wagon tongues.

A burly man in a city suit and narrow-brimmed bowler was supervising the work. Seeing big Jim Jackson, and having anticipated the sheriff's arrival, the man walked out and extended his hand.

"Sheriff Cody?" he asked.

"Yes, sir," Ned answered, taking the proffered hand, surprised by the remarkably firm grip extending from the city suit. The man wore a split tail coat, but had loosened his four-in-hand tie as a token of respect to the desert heat. He appraised Cody through gold-rimmed glasses as Jackson made introductions. "This is J.W.S. Perry," the deputy said. "Sheriff Ned Cody."

Perry shouted to a man lounging in the shade of a water wagon. "Delemeter!" The tall, slender, angular-faced man got slowly to his feet, spitting a long stream of tobacco juice from under a light-colored handlebar mustache. He ambled up the ramp to join the waiting men. With the back of his hand he wiped a bit of brown spittle from his mustache onto his overall, then extended the hand to Cody.

"Pleased, Sheriff."

"Good to meet you, Mr. Delemeter," Ned said, shaking the man's rawboned, sun-bronzed hand. "I understand you're missin' twenty or so mules."

"Eighteen head of the finest mules this side of the Mississippi," Delemeter said in disgust. "And two sixteen hand, broad-chested bay geldings. Sure hope that fellow don't split those spans up. Those are the finest teams a man could ask for."

"Do they carry a company mark?" Ned asked.

Delemeter shook his head. "Never was much of one for brandin'. Mule's a funny creature. I never been kicked by a mule what got to know me and trust me." He grinned slyly. "I always had a helper mark 'em, that'a'way they's mad at the helper." While he talked he fished a plug out of a rear overall pocket, and bit off a large chew. "They carry a small 'H' on the right shoulder, for the Harmony Borax Works. Some of 'em have other marks on the flanks, but all have the 'H'. I sure would be obliged if'n you got those mules back, Sheriff."

"I'll do my best, Mr. Delemeter," Cody said. He shook his head, refusing the plug the man offered.

"If'n a man what took 'em left a bell on

Besty," Delemeter continued, "that's short for Best Mule — then they'll stick together. They all wore bells, but they'll follow ol' Besty an' stick together. If'n the thief gets rid of the bells so's to travel quiet, then he'll have a devil of a time. They'll go ever whichaway."

As they talked, shovels full of white gypsum continued to be thrown from the wagon to the rail car. An occasional coolie hat and flashing shovel blade made a brief appearance over the deep wagon's sides.

Ned turned to Perry. "Telegram said you fellas figure this was the work of Mangas Saragosa," Cody said. "What do we know about this man?"

Big Jim Jackson, who'd been standing back lighting up a fat black cigar, stepped forward. "You fellas are making a big thing out of this," he blustered. "I can have that dog eater's red hide tacked to the barn wall in two days."

A single hard look from Cody quieted Jackson. Then, "You were saying?" the sheriff asked Perry.

"Delemeter here has met up with him a few times. I have never, thank God." Perry gave Ned a stem look though his thin-rimmed glasses. "Those animals are worth fifteen, maybe twenty thousand dollars,

Sheriff. This is a big thing to us. More serious than even a stage or bank robbery to this town. Borax provides a lot of jobs here. It's the mainstay of our economy. The company wants 'em back, and there's a reward." He touched the brim of his narrow city hat. "Excuse me," he said and went back to directing several Chinese with the off-loading.

The mule skinner removed his hat and mopped his thinning pate with a kerchief. "Saragosa used to pack a little wood down to us at the Badwater," he said. "At the sound end of Death Valley, where the Harmony is. A big broad shouldered fella. Real quiet. Some said he was a Mojave Indian. Carries a lot of tattoo marks on his back. I haven't seen him in a couple of years."

"What kind of marks?" Ned asked.

"Big ones." Delemeter measured two inches between his thumb and forefinger. "You won't miss 'em if'n you see 'em. He's drawed on like a Navajo basket from his neck to his heels. He sat at our fire a few times, an' never caused us no trouble 'til he had some problems down near the Colorado."

"Problems?"

"Heard 'bout some Mexican miners at some foreigner's mine a number of years

36

back . . . think it was called the Fleur-de-lis or some such. Anyways, they got to hoorahin' an' got a little carried away. They . . . they killed his family and most of his tribe." The tall mule skinner embarrassedly kicked at a clod of dirt. "You know how those fellas are down there. A lot of 'em still have Indian slaves, law or no law. I read a poster from down that way. Said Mangas Saragosa was wanted for killin' seven miners. They was in real bad shape when they was found."

"That was a little over a year ago," Ned offered, nodding his head. "I've seen that poster. That's why I came myself." Ned had read the poster with interest months before. He turned to Big Jim Jackson. "Where are Ratzlaff and Cuen?" the sheriff asked.

"They got in yesterday on the afternoon train. I got 'em a couple of Shoshones for guides, and they rode out. Said to tell you they didn't want the trail to get cold. I shoulda gone myself. We could have had this boy all trussed up an' waitin' in my little jail."

"Damn them! They should have waited!" Cody shook his head in disgust. "Where are the fellows who brought this wagon in?"

"Frenchy's Saloon. They've hardly left there since they got here. They was pretty shook up." Jackson smiled. "Hope they're sober enough to talk."

Ned turned to face the rawboned mule skinner who had hooked this thumbs into the straps of his overalls. "Thanks, Delemeter. Tell your boss I'll get his mules back."

"They belong to him," Delemeter spat a stream of brown tobacco, hitting a black stink bug that had paused to raise his backside in disdain, "but they's my mules. But I'll tell him."

Ned touched his hat brim, then led Big Jim Jackson down the ramp. He stopped at the bottom hearing Delemeter call after them. The lanky mule skinner took the time to spit another long stream of tobacco juice and seemed to consider what he was going to say before speaking in a low, cautious voice.

"You ought to know," he said, eyeing Cody skeptically. "Now I don't cotton to such things as a rule . . . but they say this Saragosa is more'n a man. They call him the Demon of the Desert. Not just the white folks either. Most red men call him that too. You fellas keep a sharp eye and a hand on those Colts. If he can't shoot you, he'll starve ya down 'til he picks his teeth with your bones."

Delemeter looked Cody straight in the eye. "Saragosa moves through the desert, summer or winter, like he don't need food nor water. Just cause he heads somewhere, don't think you can follow. If he is a man, he's a different kinda man. He's not like us." Delemeter tipped his hat, turned, and wandered back down the far side of the ramp into the shade of the water wagon.

Ned stood quietly watching the man go. Normally, Ned would have laughed at such a warning, but Delemeter seemed a straight talkin' man.

When Delemeter was out of earshot, Jackson laughed sarcastically. "That damned fool! More'n a man! Why that red nigger is hardly a man a'tall. That Delemeter would piss down your back and tell you it was rainin'!"

Ignoring the remark, Cody slapped Big Jim on the back smartly, raising up a cloud of desert dust. "Let's find those other fellows and see what else we can learn," he suggested.

"We don't need nothing," Jackson blustered, "but a little time and hard ridin'. In fact, you can go on back to the valley if'n you want to. I can handle this alone. Cuen and Ratzlaff'll just get in my way. I'll have that Indian —"

"Let's go see what we can learn," Cody interrupted coldly as he mounted and reined away, leaving Jackson muttering to himself, munching on his big, now soggy, black cigar.

Far out in the desolate wasteland, a grizzled prospector shaded his eyes with a calloused hand, squinting as he stepped out from the narrow shaft, surveying the rock escarpment below. His vision wandered out onto the mesquite and desert holly-covered alluvial plain spreading out for two miles beyond the escarpment to a wide sand wash bottom, then rising up again to a range of hard-shouldered basalt mountains.

He covered the mine opening with a bushy mesquite branch and pushed a few mesquite branches into the small pile of tailings that had accumulated below. Then he picked up a bucket and spread the last of the day's tailings along the game trail as he returned to his tent in the desert two hundred feet beneath him. He was careful to conceal his work, for he'd never filed a claim nor had any intention of doing so. The chance of someone stumbling on his mine deep into the Mojave Desert was slim. But still it never hurt to be careful.

Moving down the steep trail, his wheezy voice echoed against the rock wall, "Amazing grace, how sweet the whatever," he sang, "that saved the wretch like me." Unsure of the words, he made them up as he went along. He cackled to himself. It had been a good day at the end of a good month's work. Now for the reward at the end of the toil. Day after tomorrow, God willin' and the creek don't rise — and there was damn little chance of *that* — he'd soon be deep in a corn husk mattress.

He whistled shrilly for his burro. The animal brayed in answer and came trotting out of the brush. The old man pulled a canvas pack from the crotch of a mesquite, wiped the animal's back clean with one hand, then fit the canvas in place. He paused to scratch lovingly between the burro's long ears before loading his few utensils and the last of the flour and coffee on the animal. There was just enough for the trip back to civilization, if the rough town of Mojave could be called that.

As Cody and Jackson trotted the horses back to the center of town, Ned wondered and worried about his other two deputies. Theo Ratzlaff had been with him ever since the days Cody was the city marshal of Bakersfield. Theo had been a deputy with the marshal's office when Ned was first appointed. In fact, Theo figured he himself would be the one to get the marshal's job and it had taken him a long time to get over the insult. But when Cody was appointed county sheriff, he insisted on bringing Ratzlaff along — with a raise in pay of course — and Theo's attitude had changed drastically. He had always been a good deputy. Now he was a good friend as well.

Theo had been born to Russian Orthodox farmers living northwest of Bakersfield. Even taller and broader than Ned, Theo filled a room as completely as Big Jim Jackson. And he could whip most men with only one hand — which was a good thing since, right before Ned had been appointed county sheriff, Ratzlaff, Cody, and Cuen came up against a slimy owlhoot named Johnny Tenkiller, and the encounter earned Ratzlaff a load of buckshot in his right shoulder. The shoulder still wasn't working one hundred percent, but Ratzlaff had learned to shoot left-handed, and was now about as good as he'd ever been.

Alvarado Cuen's family had been in California for generations. His father had been a Don and the old title has passed on to Al, though he shunned it now. Behind his back, the Californios of Kern County still referred to him as Don Alvarado Cuen. His heritage showed in the way he sat astride his favorite stallion and in his proud, yet polite manner. Ned had hired him on as a county deputy after he had helped out in the same Tenkiller gun fight that had made Theo Ratzlaff ambidextrous.

In fact, if it hadn't been for Cuen, Cody and Ratzlaff would both be toes up in the bone yard. Cuen was a *vaquero* — as handy with a whip and knife as he was with a shotgun. Cody still hadn't been able to get the man to wear a sidearm. Cuen just figured he was better with his bullsnake whip than he would ever be with a revolver. And watching him wield the twenty-five feet of braided, tallowed leather, it seemed difficult logic to dispute.

He had learned his whip work driving mule teams in the mines of the Kern River diggings in Whiskey Flats, between Bakersfield and Mojave. And like all *vaqueros,* he could also use the reata like an extension of his arm. Its sixty feet of woven leather had been tallowed until it was soft as a sow's ear. Al could drop it easily over a steer running twenty-five paces in front of the *vaquero's* galloping mount, take a dally on the high horn of his Visalia saddle, jerk the stallion to a sliding halt, and be astride the kicking steer, brand, doctor, or three-legged tie it and be back in the saddle before the dust even settled. Though nowhere near as big as Ratzlaff, he was as tough as boot leather and as quick as a rattler.

Still, rugged as his men were, Ned couldn't help worrying about them. There never was a man a Colt or Winchester couldn't bring down to size.

Especially in the hands of a desperate backshooter.

CHAPTER THREE

Sarah McKinnes perched, near naked, on the edge of the bed.

She entwined her fingers and stretched her long slender arms out in front of her, forcing her full breasts together. Her long auburn hair fell between her eye-catching cleavage. Clad only in lace pantalettes, she stretched her willowy legs and ran her hands over her thighs, studying Frenchy for his reaction. Noticing none, she shook her head and sighed. She'd been around Frenchy too long, Sarah figured. By rights she should have headed out for San Francisco long ago. It had been three years since she'd first left Galveston, working her way toward what was reputed to be the West's most beautiful city.

The slender, fine-featured Frenchman who owned Frenchy's Saloon stood staring out the window, unmindful of her feline movements. Frenchy LeConte watched the two large lawmen walking their horses down the main street. He hurried from the window and opened the door, yelling into the hallway. "King! Get back here" The footfalls of a big man echoed through the hall and soon a massive figure filled the doorway.

King Hansen was big, rock-hard, dog-dumb, and butt-ugly and he worked for and — only God knew why — worshipped Frenchy LeConte.

Frenchy walked back to the window and pointed below at the riders dismounting and tying their horses to the hitching rail. "Isn't that the county sheriff?" the saloon owner asked.

King reluctantly pulled his pig-like eyes away from Sarah as she modestly covered herself with the bed sheet and joined Frenchy at the window. "I'll be damned if it's not," he said grinning. "He stood us all to a drink about a year ago when he was politickin'!" Bending down, King leaned his huge knuckles on the sill of the open window. "Howdy, Sheriff!" he called.

"No! No!" Frenchy snapped, pushing him out of the way. "You imbecile! Don't call attention to us! *Sacreblue!* You are an idiot!"

King stood to the side, his initial wolf-like stance eased and melted into hurt. "But he was a real nice fella, Frenchy," the big man whined. "He stood us all to a drink."

"You get down to the saloon and see if you can help clean up," Frenchy ordered. "Tell Tucker I will be down shortly."

After King left the room, Frenchy went to a low chest of drawers, filled the ivory-colored basin perched upon it with water from a matching pitcher, and slicked back his hair. He carefully waxed his mustache, checking it in the mirror, then picked up a finely polished pair of black boots from a wicker-back chair and sat on the edge of the bed to pull them on.

Dressing, he thought of the law. The last thing he needed was more of it in Mojave. Deep in thought, he continued to ignore Sarah who cocked a leg up on the chair and began pulling on and adjusting a pair of black silk stockings, rolling them down over her shapely limbs to a mid-thigh garter.

Frenchy buttoned his pin-striped waist-coat over a ruffled shirt, then slipped a little pearl-handled pepperbox into one vest pocket and a gold watch into the other, hooking its gold fob across to the pocket concealing the deadly midget gun. He patted the pepperbox. This is law enough, he thought. He carefully tied a black four-in-hand.

As if it wasn't bad enough living in a dried

out hole like Mojave, now he had to put up with more law. He could handle that stupid loud mouthed oaf, Jackson. But this sheriff might be something else. He might end up having to feed him to King. Frenchy wondered if the sheriff was here to raise the ante. He'd been paying Jackson off every month — some for the deputy and some for the boss, the sheriff in Bakersfield. Just like it had always been. But now the take was way down, so the percentage he paid Jackson was less than half what it had been a few months ago. Was that why the sheriff was here?

Frenchy cursed under his breath. He hated the unknown.

Frenchy was tired of this place, this town, this desert. There was only one thing LeConte wanted more than to get back to New Orleans — and that was getting his hands on old Polecat Pete's Poontang mine.

Unfortunately, no one knew where Pete's mine was.

Another unknown.

Old Pete came into town around the first of every month, cashed in his dust, banked some, then went straight to Cautious Callie's whore house with at least two ounces of gold. Callie had seven girls, and old Pete always stayed until he did them all. Before the town had quieted down, she'd had twelve, and Pete's stays in town could last up to three days. It didn't take long before his mine got its present nickname — The Poontang.

Frenchy growled under his breath as he silently repeated Pete's favorite saying: *What's gold good for 'cept payin' for poontang.*

Noticing Sarah had dressed, Frenchy turned to face her for the first time. "You get on down there and stir up some business. *Cherie,*" he ordered. "Things have been too slow. Get out on the street if you have to."

Sarah pouted. "That deputy Jackson said he was going to take us to jail if we worked on the streets, Frenchy," she complained. "I don't want to spend no time in that crummy jail."

"I'll handle Jackson," Frenchy said, his snarl slightly straightening the curls of his waxed mustache. "Just get some business in here." He shooed her out the door. "Put a little more rouge on your cheeks. And color those lips, *Cherie.*" He went back to his own primping, his mind still on Pete's gold.

Half the town had tried to follow old Pete when he headed back into the desert, but most of them came back empty handed.

Some didn't come back at all. And no one knew whether to rightly blame the desert, or Pete.

Pete had been too smart to file a claim. He would have had to let the world know its whereabouts, and Pete didn't exactly crave the company of a thousand scratching, thieving, claim-jumping, drunken neighbors. Still, Frenchy thought, there had to be a way. Pete was too smart to gamble. Otherwise Frenchy could have cheated him out of the property long ago on the crooked tables the Frenchman ran. But Pete went to Callie's, spent the best part of two days there, then went to the Silver Gunsight Saloon for one drink of Who Hit John, then to Frenchy's for one shot of Napoleon brandy, for which he paid the outrageous sum of two dollars and fifty cents, two days pay for an ordinary working man. He then packed up his burro and headed out once more.

Pete wasn't really much for towns, and town wasn't much for him. Pete didn't exactly get the nickname Polecat because he smelled like a rose. But the girls at Callie's didn't seem to mind. The first time Pete had come in, they'd charged him double because of his stench, and he'd been paying double ever since. To this day he still hadn't had a bath. He claimed he hated to waste the water.

And Frenchy hated Pete — because he stank, because he could afford all the women at Callie's. And Callie, who hated card cheats, would not let Frenchy near the premises. But most of all, LeConte hated Pete because Pete had a gold mine. Because Frenchy wanted to go back to New Orleans, and he wanted to go back rich. Pete's gold mine could make Frenchy richer than any man in the splendid gulf coast city which reminded him of Paris, more than any other place on this continent.

Frenchy made up his mind for the hundredth time to find Pete's claim. Pete had very nearly seen the last of his beloved poontang and Napoleon brandy. It was time for the old, one-blanket, one-burro, hardrock miner to give up his bones to the desert.

Frenchy's Saloon faced Main Street — a deep, narrow fronted drinking establishment, the height of whose ceiling only made it seem even more narrow. The mirror-lined bar stood at the back. The single row of square tables and ladder-backed chairs lined the wall across from the bar, while the rear of the saloon was jammed with rectangular faro and oblong roulette tables. The walls sported photographs of European sights done in the recently invented halftone process. Frenchy's favorites were a shot of the Arc de Triomphe and a few poorly printed posters advertising the Paris Theater. A full-figured, scantily-clad reclining blond in a tattered oil painting looked out over the saloon from a spot just high enough on the wall to be out of reach of the drunken, grasping clientele. The tin-patched board floor was littered with peanut shells, dirt, and the occasional out-of-place whiteness of a crushed egg shell.

The fat bartender, Tucker Parks, leaned casually on the bar. A barrel-chested man with a full handlebar mustache and one ear — thanks to a Paiute brave who though he was good enough to drink in Frenchy's and demonstrated an extraordinary deftness with a blade to prove it — Tucker had a belly that pushed out over his belt causing his buckle to stare directly down at the floor. He, a local drunk, Sarah McKinnes, and the skinner and swamper from the borax were the saloon's only occupants — not counting Winky, the piano player and permanent saloon fixture. Winky was perched at his usual spot, in front of the upright against the back wall next to the rear door of the saloon. The piano sat in that strategic location so Winky — who normally couldn't see over three feet in front of his face — could make sure no one decided to tote a mug, glass, chair, table, or Sarah out of the place. His less-than-proficient piano playing was continually interrupted by his loud arguments with customers who felt compelled to carry their mugs out to the necessary thirty feet from the back door. A few months earlier, after numerous complaints about the warmer-than-usual beer, one of the boys thought it would be a big joke to sweeten a mug with some processed "beer" out in the necessary room and exchanged it for Tucker's. One warm, salty sip, and Tucker went crazy. He tore the bar to pieces, breaking chair and tables while retiring two patrons to their beds for a week. Thus the rule: No Mugs Outside — not that anyone seriously considered trying that again.

Cody and Jackson shoved their way through the swinging doors.

"Jim," the big bartender called waving. "Want a beer?"

"Too early for me, Tucker," Big Jim answered coldly. "Sheriff here wants to chew the fat with those borax boys." Tucker Parks stared quizzically at Jackson. It wasn't like the deputy to turn down a beer.

Tucker leaned his belly against the bar and grinned broadly at Cody. "Fat's better with a beer chaser, Sheriff," he said rubbing the stub of his ear with a bar towel. "How about it? It's on the house."

"A little early for me," Cody refused, touching his hat brim in recognition. "Thanks anyway."

The fat man shrugged as Cody and Jackson made their way to the table where the two skinners were working on a bottle of Black Widow whiskey. Winky plunked away, delivering his own unique rendition of *Buffalo Gal* on the upright.

Cody extended his hand. A gray-eyed man with a full salt and pepper beard focused on Cody's star, then stood, swaying drunkenly. He leaned one hand on the table top for support, reaching out and taking Cody's offered hand with the other.

"I'm Sheriff Cody from Bakersfield," Ned told them. "You the fellas who had the trouble?"

"I'm Thad Spencer," the tall, sallow faced man replied, rocking on his feet dangerously. "And this here's Horace Trumbell." He motioned toward his table-mate. "His cousin, Dallas, was one of the men what got shot."

"Sorry about that, Mr. Trumbell."

The seated man looked up through bleary, bloodshot eyes. "T' weren't your fault Sheriff," he said quietly. "I tol' Dallas we shoulda light a shuck for home. He would never listen."

Cody pulled up a chair and sat. Jackson left his side and walked to the bar, where the bartender handed him a foam-capped beer. The deputy drank surreptitiously, keeping his broad back to Cody.

"What happened?" Cody asked the skinner and swamper.

"Jud McGrath." Spencer answered, retaking his seat as gingerly as possible for a man in his condition, "was driving the second wagon. I was driving the first. I heard a shot, then another about as fast as a man could lever in. I couldn't see the trailing wagon so's I yelled at Horace here. He's a swamper same as Dallas was. Anyways, I yelled at Horace here to pull up, and I jumped down. By the time I hit the ground and got to where I could see, both Jud and Dallas was lyin' on the ground. I started to run back to 'em, but the bushwhacker took a shot at me. I looked up into those rocks and this big fella was standing up, waving his rifle and screamin' like a banshee."

"Was the shot close?" Cody asked.

"Kicked up gravel all over me," Spencer

said, wide-eyed. "I dove back behind the water wagon, and Horace here joined me."

Horace had dropped his head to the table. At the mention of his name he raised it a bit, but then returned it to the table top with a hollow thump.

"Anyways," Spencer continued, "we waited awhile. Old Jud only kicked one time, then neither of them moved. I figgered they was a dead as a rock. I had a wagon gun, an old .50/.70 Springfield. But I ain't no gunfighter." He downed another shot then refilled his glass. "Finally, after a half hour we crawled back to 'em. Both of 'em was head shot with the flies already blowin' 'em. The nearest cover was a rock pile. It musta been about two hundred yards."

Thad Spencer threw down his shot glass full of three fingers of the dark whiskey. "Damnedest shootin' I ever saw," he went on. "I was real lucky, real lucky. I figger if that man wanted to hit me, he would have."

"What did you do then?" Cody asked. He waited patiently while the man filled yet another shot glass full. But this time Spencer sipped at the liquor. Another big man entered the bar and crossed to where Jackson, still talked quietly with the bartender. Cody eyed the man while he waited for Spencer to continue. The newcomer's squinty eyes were lost in a head the size of a powder keg. He must have topped three hundred pounds, even bigger than the massive Jackson. Thad Spencer yelled for the bartender to bring another bottle, and Cody dug out a dollar to pay for it. An auburn-haired girl brought it to the table. She eyed Cody up and down, appraising him shamelessly.

"Anything else, Sheriff?" she cooed. "Anything at all?" She stood saucily with her hands on her hips.

"No, thank you." Ned smiled, returning her look appreciatively. He then turned his attention back to the business at hand. Spencer continued with his story as the girl flounced back to the bar.

"Obliged, Sheriff," the skinner said, acknowledging the bottle. "Well, we figgered the fella must want the stock. Don't you go tellin' Delemeter or Perry this, but we cut 'em loose figgerin' it was better he got the mules than Horace and me.

He threw down the rest of the shot. "Then we hightailed it out of there. I kept lookin' back at that rock pile — borax wagon ain't exactly no race horse — an' caught a glimpse of that Indian. I guess he was an Indian. He had hair to the middle of his back. He stood up atop a rock, watchin' us leave. An' that's all I saw."

Cody stood and tipped his hat to the two men. As he walked to the door, he called to Jackson, who quickly downed the remains of his second beer, wiped his mouth with one of the towels that hung by the bar and rushed to join the sheriff at the swinging doors.

Outside, Jackson mounted his horse as Cody tightened the cinch he'd previously loosened. "You said Cuen and Ratzlaff had two Shoshone guides?" he asked, raising his head. "How about for us?"

"They's two more waitin' for us at the livery, Cody," Jackson snorted derisively. "But I don't need 'em. I know this desert."

"Well, I don't," Cody replied harshly. "We may have to split up along the way." Cody was beginning to wonder if the man would ever get the slack out of his tongue.

"We might as well get on with it," Cody was frowning. He was uncomfortable with the fact that Cuen and Ratzlaff had gone on ahead. And being saddled with Jackson was beginning to make him uncomfortable as well.

As they plodded along the dusty streets, Cody looked the town over. Mojave seemed haphazardly planned by men in a hurry to get on with the work at hand. Boardwalks lined the street side before a few false-fronted buildings. Tents stood between some board and batt buildings. Most of the structures were boarded up. An occasional masonry building testified to someone's naïve belief in the future of the town. But most of these were vacant as well.

The horses kicked the deep dust of the street in billows out in front of these as they walked. The fine dust rose up to cover the riders long before they had time to get clear of it. They rode up to a clapboard building with a sign announcing "Elroy's Livery". Two Indians rose from their haunches from where they had been squatting in the shade. A paint horse and a large dappled gray were ground-tethered close by m the shade of a tamarack tree.

"Cody," Jackson said pointing a thick finger at the Indians. "The big one is Two's Riding and the little one is Yellow Hair."

Cody stared curiously at the smaller man. His hair was as coal black and stringy as the first, but the sheriff said nothing, merely touched his hat brim. The chisel-faced, nut brown men stood motionless, not acknowledging the greeting. They both wore heavy, loose-fitting shirts, canvas trousers tucked into leather leggings, moccasins, and wide-brimmed, un-creased hats. Rope belts, encircled their waists. The one Jackson had introduced as Two's Riding gathered up an old, heavy barreled .50 caliber Sharps that leaned against the building. Both Indians carried homemade long knives in their belts. Saying nothing, they disappeared into the livery.

"They gotta get the pack mule," Jackson explained. "Your water bag full up?"

"Yep," Cody answered. A bedroll, canvas sack, and canteen were tied securely on the back of his saddle.

The two braves reappeared shortly with a big Roman-nosed mule in tow. Leather-trimmed canvas packs hung from a mesquite pack saddle, and a bag of rolled oats topped off the load. Without a word, Two's Riding heaved a two-gallon water bag up, and strapped it behind Cody's bedroll. Ned nodded to the man. "Thanks," he said.

The Indian merely grunted. He swung up into his saddle without the aid of its carved wooden stirrups. The one called Yellow Hair looked Cody up and down. "Need heavy shirt!" the redman insisted. Cody's light cotton shirt was already plastered to his body with sweat.

"Won't this one do?" Cody asked. "I got a flannel one in the bedroll." Ned was hesitant to put on anything heavier in the already intolerable heat.

"Need heavy shirt," the Indian repeated.

"Reluctantly, Cody dismounted, pulling off the water bag and canteen to get to the bedroll. He removed the flannel shirt and stripped off the saturated light one. It was their country, and Cody had learned long ago the worth in watching, listening and learning. Both the Indians and Jackson were already dressed in long sleeved heavy garments.

The Indians reined in their horses and the four riders started off into the desert. It was just before noon, and the blistering desert heat was already torturing Ned's back and lathering the horses and mule, sending rivulets of dust-muddy foam cascading down their withers and chests. Ned removed his hat and wiped his brow with the red kerchief. They had only been outside for a few minutes and already his hat was sweated through.

They passed the last shack, leaving the safety of Mojave behind. Far in the distance lakes of illusion danced, disappeared, and then almost as quickly reappeared.

Cody scanned a horizon as broad as his imagination could conjure up. He wondered how many places there were out there where a man could hide.

A hundred thousand.
A million for a demon.

Chapter Four

Mangas Saragosa sat on a low ridge, cradling his Henry rifle as he watched his back trail.

He had covered over twenty miles since stealing the mules and horses. The wiry, spotted mustang Mangas rode was as swift as the desert wind and the horse was hardly blowing by the time the Indian had rounded up the stock after the swamper had cut them free. Saragosa left the bells on four mules including the one that had been the lead jenny, and drove them all into the desert away from the narrow, pitted trail that passed for a road.

Stock meant money and money was something Saragosa had learned was necessary for getting along in the white man's world. Though it was a world he wanted no part of, the intruders kept forcing it on him. More and more they were everywhere, like sand in the desert. Saragosa knew he would have to make the best of it and take the best of it. As they had taken the best of his life from him.

Mangas sat in the shade of a smoketree leaning back against its roughly gnarled trunk. His broad, smoke-brown face seemed at peace under a red tightly bound cotton headband as he dozed in the heat of the afternoon. His wide flaring nostrils tested the air with each quiet breath, his ears remained on constant alert for any sound other than the buzzing and clicking of insects.

He'd gathered the stock in a tight circle at the foot of a steep cliff, at the base of which a seep trickled forming a saltgrass encircled, shaded pool. Enough soil had formed from the decaying saltgrass through which a few brave shoots of sweet grass fought valiantly for life. Mangas allowed the mules and horses to water, rest and feed as best they could.

The long, steep canyon falling away below him sheltered a winding flat sand bottom, one that would flood deeply and treacherously when the mountains were blessed with — or ravished by — rain. The canyon rose steely with walls of red rock broken by an occasional slash of brown basalt. Its familiarity took Mangas back to another time and another canyon.

When he was young, before he wore the tattoos of a warrior, his father had tried to make peace with the white man. A group of miners had moved into a canyon — not unlike the one in which he presently dozed — not far from his father's village. The Indians had had problems with the men who came to work the hills. These men hunted game, which was natural, but then left behind the head, hide, and entrails. Deer and antelope that would have fed and clothed and made tools for the whole tribe were abandoned to rot in the desert sun.

The clumsy miners drove the game far away from the canyon. A small clash between the miners and the Indians had left one miner wounded. But the miners sent a peacemaker, and the peacemaker invited the Indians to the miner's camp. They would smoke the pipe of peace and eat meals in friendship. There would be presents for the Indians — knives of shiny metal and sticks that speak and kill the swift-moving deer and antelope.

All the men, women, and children of the village — over fifty in all — came to gather around the miner's cooking fires. The miners sang and entertained the Indians, giving them plenty of *aguardiente* to drink. The guests didn't notice as the miners slowly began disappearing from the camp. The Indians stayed behind to eat, smoke and play games with the children.

Since the camp had been erected beside a small muddy stream running through a steep, unscalable canyon, when the miners opened fire there was nowhere to run. The miners sang as they cut the throats of the wounded. Only twelve Indians escaped — ten women, one older boy, and Mangas. The muddy stream darkened even more with the blood of his fallen people. His father, mother, and two older brothers had fallen to the miner's treachery. The echoes of the white man's singing stayed with Mangas for years. He dreamed of it often.

Later, the women who had survived the massacre were captured while the boys hunted. Years afterward, Mangas learned the women had been taken to Mexico to be sold as slaves.

The older boy was killed in a fall while robbing a swallow's nest on a steep cliff. So Mangas, at fifteen, was forced to live alone in the desert. He stayed alone for two years, then, desperate for human company, he joined another tribe who spoke his language. The Mojaves were a tough clan of desert traders who made Mangas prove himself before he could earn the tattoos of the warrior. But earn them he did, before a single year had passed.

He returned to the miner's camp time and time again, killing and mutilating seven of them over the next two years. Mangas had not even been sure if the men he killed were the ones responsible for the death of his people. But by that time it no longer mattered. In Saragosa's eyes, all white men were to blame. It reached a point where no one would leave the camp without two heavily armed escorts. His bloodlust satisfied for the time being, Mangas Saragosa had moved deeper into the desert.

Saragosa snapped instantly alert and fully awake. A dull red, flat-bodied chuckwalla scampered across a nearby rock. Saragosa watched the lizard disappear into a crevice. The heavy-shouldered, muscular Indian — older by far than his young years would indicate — stood up, leaving the shade of the smoketree, and padded over to a creosote bush. He selected the straightest of its two foot branches, quickly stripped it and split the end with his long blade knife. Finding a small, sharp-edged stone, he inserted it into the split, then bound it securely with thin strips of bark so the stone formed a hook at the end of the stick.

Silently, he crept back to the crevice where the chuckwalla had disappeared. Two feet deep and just wide enough for the reptile's flat body, the crevice would normally have been a safe hiding place. If Mangas was not mouse-careful and owl-silent, the lizard would expand his body, wedging himself into the crack, making himself impossible to remove. Slowly Mangas eased the creosote branch down into the crevice. Before the chuckwalla could realize that he was in danger, Mangas hooked the stone into the soft flesh of its underbelly, and flipped the lizard out, catching him in midair. One lizard would enable Mangas to go another twenty-four hours without a meal just as long as he had water. And Mangas knew every water hole between Mojave and the Colorado.

His medicine bag held a few charms, a few peyote pods, and a steel and flint for making fires. He shaved some fine strands of dry mesquite and struck the flint to steel. Sparks caught on the first try, and he built a small fire in the pile of dry wood. What little smoke there was dissipated completely, long before climbing above the canyon.

Saragosa gutted and skewered the lizard. After he'd roasted and eaten his meal, gnawing even the tough skin and fine bones and swallowing them down, Mangas climbed high onto the face of the cliff. He shaded his eyes, and watched. Far below and still far away, four men on horseback leading a pack animal rode close to the entrance of the canyon. Their legs seemed to disappear in the shimmering heat, then their torsos, until their heads and calves seemed to be traveling detached. But still they came. They always came. And Mangas always killed them.

This time would be no different.

Alvarado Cuen followed fifty feet behind the Shoshone guides, trying to avoid their dust. He hummed a Mexican tune, occasionally breaking into full-voiced song. His white cotton shirt was clinging to him, brown with dirt and sweat. Gray salt stains lined the armpits and neck. A black leather vest supporting gleaming silver conchos and rawhide ties hung loose. His breeches, *calzonevas,* were embroidered down the outside seam with conchos catching and reflecting the gold of the sun.

Theo Ratzlaff rode directly behind him, only breaking his personal silence with an occasional grunt, curse, or comment about Al's singing.

Theo reined up beside Cuen. "My throat's

so dry I'm spittin' dust," the big man complained in a low gravel voice.

"You don't need to worry about being quiet, my friend." Al looked at his partner from under his own broad-brimmed *sombrero*. "If this Saragosa doesn't know we come, then he is a blind man."

"He's just another damned, ugly, bad-breathed dog eater." Theo growled, slapping at a small desert bee that buzzed about his sweaty brow. "Even if he knows we're coming, we're going to nail his ugly butt. "I'll bet the borax works will pay a pretty penny to get their stock back." Theo removed his floppy-brimmed Palo Alto hat and ran a hand through his thinning hair. He took another angry swipe at the pestering bee with the Palo Alto before returning the hat to his head.

"At least you could have brought a decent hat, *amigo.*" Alvarado said, his smile curving one side of his mouth. "The next time we come into the desert, I will get you a fine *sombrero* like mine. Maybe a black one with silver threads." Ratzlaff was so big that the floppy broad-brimmed hat he wore looked tiny.

"No thanks, *amigo,*" Theo grunted. "I don't want nobody thinkin' I'm related to you. It's bad enough a farm boy like me, hungry an' thirsty as I am havin' to be out here with two dog eaters an' a greas— an' a chili pepper." Theo knew Al hated being called a greaser. He also was aware that Alvarado Cuen would fight at the drop of a hat — *sombrero* or otherwise. Theo had fought him only once, back when he had two good shoulders. To date, the Californio Cuen had been the only man ever to knock huge Theo Ratzlaff to the ground. After that day they'd come to an unspoken truce — Theo didn't call Al "greaser" and Al didn't call Ratzlaff "rat", as his name so freely gave invitation to do.

"Theo," Al said quietly, slightly miffed at Theo's near-gaffe. "You better hope those 'dog eaters' don't take a fancy to fat 'farm boy'. You look cooked, done to a medium rare turn." Al laughed. His perfect teeth gleamed extra white against is nut-brown face. Then all of a sudden, he turned serious again.

"I am getting a little worried about the water situation," Cuen said. "Finding water in the desert is difficult enough, even for these Shoshones. Fallowing a man like Saragosa — if that's who it is we're following — makes it double tough, *amigo.* He will poison the water holes if he has a means to, and you will have to drink this bottle of *aguardiente* I have in my bedroll." The trail steepened as the horses hoofs clattered noisily on the rocks.

"I wouldn't drink that horse piss you *cholos* drink even if'n my stomach was dried tight to my backbone." Theo's smile abruptly changed to a grimace as his horse slipped, nearly falling to its knees. "Goddamn! Don't be goin' down on me, horse. It's a long walk home."

The two guides stopped long enough for Al and Theo to catch up. The Indians were grandfather and grandson. The elder's peach-pit face was as lined and creviced and as brown as the walls of the canyon they followed. The younger, respecting his grandfather's age and wisdom, hadn't said a word since they'd left Mojave. They'd ridden most of the night, sleeping only a few hours in the coolest part of the predawn morning. The old man didn't like to travel in the heat, but he had read the sign and knew Saragosa was pushing hard.

The old man dismounted slowly in the shade of a steep cut in the canyon wall. "He is very close," he said, squatting and motioning his grandson to dismount. "We wait here."

Theo's mouth fell open in surprise. "We hired you to guide us," he bellowed angrily.

72

"And by God, guide us you will!"

"We wait here," the old man repeated firmly, remaining motionless.

"What is the trouble, *Viejo?*" Al asked, getting down from his own horse and sitting cross-legged in front of the old Indian.

"We paid to track," the man replied using sign language to embellish his words. "I not give my spirit to the spirit of the dead. We have no fight with Mangas Saragosa. No fight with spirit of the dead."

"Spirits don't leave no tracks, old man," Ratzlaff argued, but sensed discussion was hopeless.

Al looked up at the mounted deputy and shrugged his shoulders.

Theo pointed up the rugged draw. "What if we don't find him up there?" he asked.

"You will not find him," the old man said quietly. "But he is there. He may find you. We wait here. When you not find him, you come back. Then we track again."

Theo shook his head in disgust. "Well, if that don't beat all," he muttered. "I got no hankerin' to ride all the way back here. I'll shoot three times when we get him an' you bring the pack horse on up to pack out the body."

"No." The old man insisted emphatically. "You come back. Shots mean you dead. We not come."

"Well, hell!" Theo exclaimed as Cuen mounted up, pulling his Winchester .44/40 from its saddle scabbard. He levered in a shell, checked the load, then let the hammer down easily. Satisfied, he turned to Theo. "Let us get on up there and get this done," he said and started up the rise.

Theo glanced at the pack mule then turned to the younger Indian. "I'm gonna leave this pack animal with you," he snapped harshly. "If'n you leave with him, I'm gonna' skin you when I find you. And that's a promise!"

The young Indian reached out and took the lead rope, returning Theo's cold gaze but saying nothing. Theo spurred his horse and clattered off to catch up with Alvarado.

The riders were still two miles away, with over a mile of tough climbing ahead of them before the canyon flattened out near where Mangas busily crowded the mules into a tight group. The little seep pool at the cliff's base was only twelve feet across and but a few inches deep. The mules kicked and muddied the water, pissing solid streams and plopping their mess at random. By the time Mangas started driving the animals toward a branch of the ravine at the head of a second canyon the water was totally unfit for consumption. As he moved, Saragosa watched the horizon. Perhaps the men had separated. But he could see nothing. He drove the mules to a clattering run, then abandoned them, knowing they would follow the canyon until they found graze again. And Saragosa knew where that would be.

Then he turned to his back trail, and his pursuers.

CHAPTER FIVE

Ned was used to dry, unforgiving country. But the Mojave was unlike anything he had ever experienced.

The Sierra Nevadas wrung the last of the moisture from the Pacific storms long before they could moisten this desert. A good portion of water ran down from the mountains to the west into the dry valleys, but it was swallowed up before it could travel two miles into the wasteland.

"Dry" was not a strong enough word to adequately describe the country through which they rode.

High wispy clouds teased the parched landscape but brought no moisture. The winds whistled, drying lips and skin and filling eyes and mouths with grit. But they too brought no moisture. Dust devils danced macabre, swivel-hipped tangos in the distance, promising to scatter the bones of the little caravan if they were careless — but promised no moisture.

Two's Riding and Yellow Hair led the way, riding side by side, occasionally pointing at something unseen by the two following behind. The Indians never spoke, communicating everything by hand signs. The makeshift posse followed the tracks of two shod and two unshod horses. Theo Ratzlaff and Al Cuen were only hours ahead.

Though Ned had covered his face with a kerchief as soon as they left Mojave, his eyes soon filled with grit. His teeth felt like sandpaper as he ran a dry tongue across them. This country had a way of taking everything out of a man, including his conversation. Ned had already heard about enough from Jackson as he cared to for one day. And although they now found little left to talk about, that hadn't stopped Big Jim from complaining.

The country started to change drastically. The big spiny trees the Mormons had named Joshua after the prophet who raised his hands to heaven entreating his God for help were now growing sparse. Even the gray-green mesquite and creosote were now scarce. They crossed salt flats, some a mile wide and no telling how long, containing no growth whatsoever, not even saltgrass. They had to stop every hour to wet the horses' and the mule's lips with their dampened kerchiefs, and to take deep draws themselves from their water bags.

Ned, following Big Jim's example, gulped greedily. "Won't we run out of water drinkin' this often?" he asked.

Jackson shook his head. The Shoshones believe you're better off carrying water in your belly," he answered. "You'll sweat it all out but you'll sweat anyways. You got to replace what you lose. If you don't, you'll just dry up and blow away. These fellas know every water hole in this desert. Right now they're counting on the water wagon that was left behind with the borax rig. It should have a couple of hundred gallons left. Least ways that's what the skinner tol' me."

"And if it doesn't?"

"We'll be dry a ways. But Two's Ridin' will find water. He can smell it better than a burro."

They pushed on until the sun was low in the sky. The shadows of the mountains began to cross the valley. The sun had dropped below the Panamint ridge by the time they spotted the huge borax wagons in the middle of a dry wash.

Two's Riding dismounted and walked to the water wagon. The bung in its belly was swinging from its hinge. It had been opened, its precious cargo spilled onto the dry wash bed. He thumped it soundly with the butt of his Sharps, listening to its hollow echo, then climbed on top. Straddling it, the Indian pulled off the cover.

If there was no water, there'd be hell to pay.

The canyon lay deep in shadows by the time Mangas first heard the clatter of hoofbeats. He'd been crouching in the same position for over an hour in a deep, shadowy crevice overlooking the bottom of the boulder-strewn wash. Looking down into the ravine, he slowly lifted his rifle to his shoulder as the riders came into view.

Sighting down the barrel of the Henry, Saragosa drew a careful bead on the chest of the leading rider. As the man drew closer, Mangas caught the gleam of silver conchos on the black vest and the tell-tale upward curve of his *sombrero* brim. Saragosa felt his blood turning cold. A Mexican, he thought bitterly. A Mexican. Mangas hated Mexicans. Mexicans had butchered his family and Mexicans had wiped out his tribe. A clean, quick killing was too good for a Mexican.

Mangas waited.

As the riders approached, the large man

in the rear reined up beside the Mexican, then took the lead. Mangas worked his way through the rocks until he was directly above where the riders would pass.

He pressed himself flat against a boulder a few feet above the rutted bed of the dry stream as the riders clattered forward.

They drew abreast of him. Mangas suddenly sprang from the rocks. As he flew past the trailing rider, Saragosa cracked the barrel of the Henry across the hated Mexican's *sombrero.* Mangas screeched the cry of the eagle as the Mexican went crashing to the ground.

The lead horse reared back. Mangas spun around as soon as he landed, swung his rifle up and fired.

The big man went down like a rock and lay unmoving on the canyon floor. His panicking horse charged up the canyon, dragging the unconscious man behind, his head bouncing up and down on the boulder strewn sand bed, until his boot worked free of the stirrup.

The Mexican's mount surged past the gray gelding. The riderless black stallion snorted, kicking gravel out behind his powerful hooves.

The Mexican stirred, Mangas brought the heavy barrel down across the man's head a second time. Noticing the whip bound to the belt at the Mexican's back, Mangas jerked it loose and used the long woven rawhide to bind the man's arms and legs.

Saragosa padded over to the larger of the two victims, presuming him to be dead. A look of surprise crossed the Indian's face when he saw that his slug had only creased the top of the huge man's head. A deep groove replaced hair and hide from the back of his skull and the bone showed clean and white, but the man still breathed.

Mangas cocked the Henry and lay the muzzle against the man's head. He paused, then let the hammer down softly. No, he decided, these were deaths to be savored. The Mexican would fear his own death more if allowed to watch his friend die screaming in agony first.

Disarming both men, Saragosa walked up the canyon to where their horses had stopped, idling in the shade of canyon wall. Catching them easily as they stepped on their dragging reins, he led them back. Taking the lead rope from the neck of one horse, Mangas used it to bind the hands of the shot and bleeding man.

He lifted the Mexican effortlessly and tossed him across the saddle of one of the horses. The other man was more difficult.

He had almost decided to leave him behind with a bullet in his skull to discourage any more who might follow when, with one last mighty heave, he managed to heft the gargantuan body up and lay it across the saddle. A *reata* was bound to one of the saddles. Mangas cut it in half with his knife and used the two pieces to tie the two men firmly in place.

He ran up the boulder-strewn slope effortlessly and recovered his own horse, then led him back down to the canyon's bottom. Mounting, he drove the man-laden horses out in front of him.

Three miles later Saragosa came upon the place where he had known the stolen mules would stop — a wet spot where Mangas had found water previously. A half acre of green sweetgrass grew in the shade of some willows. The mules and wheel horses grazed contentedly. Saragosa dropped his captives to the ground, then tied each man to a separate willow trunk. He then mounted up once again and rode back to the canyon to make sure no one else was following.

Mangas would wait for three hours until the sun was well below the horizon and he could no longer see into the desert below. Only then would he decide it was safe to return to camp.

One rear wheel of the water wagon rested in a slight depression, tilting the wagon at an angle. The rear of the tank still held a few quarts, enough to replenish the posse's supply and get them through most of the next day. If they were careful.

The Indians unhitched the wagon, leveling it to enable the water to reach the bung in its bottom, then filled the canvas bags. Ned carefully surveyed their surroundings. The desert was beginning to take on color again as the harsh, burning sun dipped low on the horizon. He spotted a rock pile a couple of hundred yards away. With the wind whistling all around him, Cody threaded his way through low desert holly and tall clumps of arrowweed until he reached it. A sidewinder looped erratically across the sand. Cody glanced back down toward the wagon. The shooter must have been fairly high up in the rock pile. Cody climbed higher, carefully searching for sign in the failing light. Reaching a point where he could make out the low ravine-bottom road, Ned let out a low whistle. The man must be a hell of a marksman to make two head shots at that distance. "As fast as a man could lever them in," the mule skinner had said.

It was almost too dark to see now. Just as he had decided to head back down, Ned stumbled across the area where the bush-whacker had waited. The pad marks of moccasins and the depressions of knees in the sand clearly indicated where the killer had knelt. The shell casings were gone. Saragosa had been careful to take them with him. The only physical indication of his presence was a chewed root or pod of some kind resting on top of a rock. Ned stuffed the gnawed pod into his shirt pocket and started the slow walk back to camp in the darkness.

Ned could hear the crackle and smell the mouthwatering aroma of frying bacon long before he was able to see the fire. He walked into the campsite and plopped down heavily on a fireside rock. Jackson was busy opening a tin of sweet English biscuits. He pulled a bottle of Golden Rule whiskey from his bed roll and offered it to Ned. "Get the dust out of your throat?"

"No, thanks," Cody replied. "Bacon and biscuits will do me just fine." Ned removed the chewed pod from his pocket and extended it to Jackson in his open palm. "What's this?" he asked.

The deputy shrugged. "Beats me," he said.

"Yellow Hair will know. He's some kind of a tribal shaman. He knows every plant around."

The Indians had made their own camp in a nearby creosote thicket. Ned took a step toward them, then stopped and turned back to Jackson. "How'd that Indian get the name of Yellow Hair anyway?"

Big Jim smiled. "A few years back, after the Paiute and Shoshone wars, he carried a coup stick lined with yellow scalps. Looked as if some flat-headed Dutchman lost his whole family. He's probably still got them scalps in some lodge somewhere. He found out it weren't a good idea to carry them around white folks."

"No, I wouldn't think it would be," Ned agreed. He turned and worked his way through the brush. Approaching the creosote thicket he carefully called out "hello the camp," then made his way to where the Indians sat cross-legged. Cody crouched down next to them and extended the chewed pod.

"Peyote," Yellow Hair said quietly. "Saragosa. The man talks with the dead ones. He is one with them."

"What does it do for you?" Ned asked.

"It make you . . ." the Indian searched for the proper words. ". . . a spirit . . . the wind . . . a shadow . . . a hawk, or a snake, or a cougar. More, and less, than a man." Satisfied, Yellow Hair turned his attention back to his friend.

Ned continued to sit for a minute, then got up quietly. When he returned to the campfire, Jackson was forking the bacon out onto two small tin plates. Ned picked up the bottle of Golden Rule. "Don't mind if I do," he mumbled, then tilted the bottle back and took a long, deep draw.

Later, as Ned chewed slowly at his dinner, and Jackson alternated between bites of bacon and beans and long pulls on the whiskey bottle, Ned tried to conjure up an image of the man he pursued. Saragosa had already killed at least seven men, with no telling how many others. He was a man of the desert, pure and simple — a 'demon' of the desert if the Harmony Borax mule skinner, Delemeter, was to be taken at his word. He was a man who had lost his own family to killers and slavers. A man with nothing to live for. A man who used plants — peyote — that made him "more than a man."

Ned knew little about peyote, but he knew about opium. The Chinese in Bakersfield had several opium dens. "Rooms of heavenly pleasure" they called them. The Chinese thought the use of the drug would bring them closer to heaven, making them something more than mortal men.

There was one thing Ned was sure of, though. No matter how much whiskey or opium a man used, he would still fall, if peppered with enough lead. And the sheriff was certain the same held true for peyote.

At least he hoped so.

Polecat Pete jabbered continually as he walked beside the burro that had been by his sole companion for over ten years. He rubbed his slightly recessed, whisker-stubbled chin thoughtfully and glanced up at the moonless sky. "It's dark enough to be a blind man's holiday, ain't it, Moses?" he said. Then he glanced into the Joshua forest surrounding them. "Moses, what do ya think ol' boy? Are they out there tryin' to git at ol' Pete's gold again?" He paused as if waiting for the burro's answer. "Yes siree. I'm a-thinkin' so too. We'll backtrack over Squeaky Canyon and work our way through Big Thicket just more time afore we head into Callie's day after tomorrow."

The prospector grinned at his four-hooved friend. "I'm gonna get you a full gallon of the best oats, an' soak 'em in the Emperor's Tears, ol' pardner. That'll show that smart-ass frog! Callin' me Polecat! Two shots of

Napoleon brandy for me and two shots for you, darlin'."

The floppy hat Pete wore had seen over a thousand miles of desert. In his youth, Pete had been a handsome man. But the rigors of sun and sand had taken their toll. His dirty salt-and-pepper hair hung straight down from beneath his hat — which he never removed — to just above his shoulders. Pete hated the fact that the hair on the top of his head was long gone. And now his liver-spotted pate couldn't stand the sun. Pete even wore his hat to bed, the wide variety of real beds with corn husk mattresses he'd been able to plop into once a month now that he'd struck it rich a second time. The vein Pete had found was the richest he'd ever seen. The quartz outcropping in the Devil's Bowler just kept getting wider the deeper he went. And the golden veins within did the same. If Pete had been just a mite younger, he probably would have put together a mining syndicate and mined the land right. He'd done so on a find in Placer County right after the big rush, when he was still a young buck. And he'd had more than enough time to blow the money he'd made from that one. Whores in houses from Canton to Caracas to the Cape of Good Hope knew, and probably remembered, the tall, handsome gentleman called Peter William Stone. Not a one of them would recognize Polecat Pete.

Pete knew he'd never live to spend the money he'd already banked from this strike, and the most fun in life he now had was visiting Callie's. The second most fun he had was "smelling up" Frenchy LeConte's saloon. Of course, Pete realized he wouldn't even be allowed in the door if he didn't always buy a shot of the best stuff in the house.

This time he was really going to show the pompous bastard. This time he was going to take Moses in for a drink as well. It would be a treat to make a fool out of the duded-up frog.

Pete cackled and jabbered to his burro. "Come on, ol' Moses. I'm a gonna take you right inta the frog's saloon and pour you a shot of Frenchy's best brandy." The old prospector laughed and slapped at his thighs gleefully. "Course, that'll hafta wait 'til I pleasures the ladies," he added seriously. Then man and beast continued on toward the distant goal of Mojave.

Alvarado Cuen came to on his back in the darkness, his head throbbing with each beat of his heart. His hands bound behind him felt as dead as two rocks. He struggled to free himself, but gave up after several minutes realizing it was useless. Trying to stand, he rolled over onto his belly. But, being hogtied, he found that any attempt to straighten his legs resulted in choking him. The Indian had taken a turn from wrists to neck and back to ankles, he could see by straining and gazing at his legs. And the savage had used Cuen's own whip to do so.

Al squinted trying to bring his surroundings into focus. In the moonlight he saw his horse grazing with a herd of mules on the green grass nearby. Theo Ratzlaff lay bound and motionless a few feet away. "Ratzlaff!" Cuen called quietly, so as not to be overheard in case their captor was nearby. "Goddamn it, Theo, wake up."

But Theo did not move. He must have been hit awfully hard, Al thought. Then suddenly Ratzlaff moaned once and rolled to his side. But still his eyes remained closed. The ugly gash across the back of his head was raw and weeping. Dried blood caked his hair.

"Son-of-a-bitch," Al mumbled. Again he strained to free his bound hands. Since rolling off them, the feeling had begun to return. They prickled and burned like fire. At least the blood supply had not been completely cut off by the tightly bound whip.

"Su madre es un puta" Al screamed angrily, noticing his *reata* lying nearby, cut in two pieces, its frayed ends splayed across the ground. He'd had that *reata* for ten years. It had become like a third hand to him. He'd probably greased it with the tallow of five steers over the many years.

I'll have your tattooed ass for that, Al thought. Then, in the distance, Cuen heard the clattering of hoofbeats. He strained at his bound hands one more time, then closed his eyes. The deputy wasn't sure he wanted this desert Indian to know he was conscious. Not yet.

Cody had put a pot of beans on the dying fire before turning in for the night and the mesquite fire had done its duty, supplying the posse with a breakfast of cold beans and dry biscuits in the first faint light of dawn. By the time the sun had flared up in the morning sky, its brilliant orange muted by the haze and heat, the small band was back on the trail.

The tracking wasn't difficult. The trail of eighteen mules and four horses, all shod, along with three unshod horses was easy to follow as it led to the northeast across the blistering hell known as Death Valley.

Ned figured that they were close to being out of Kern County. But jurisdiction be damned, he thought. The crime had been committed in his county and the victims were from there as well. He'd worry about the jurisdiction if anyone argued the fact, an occurrence that was highly unlikely. If they weren't already, before long they would be in Inyo County. Hell, Ned thought as they plodded along, Inyo was where his old friend Henry Hammer hung his spurs. Wouldn't it be something to run into the black Indian fighter again. Ned could certainly use his help. But Henry, if he wasn't north in Mono County, would likely be in Bishop at the very north end of Inyo. And the chance of running into him — or any other human being in this God forsaken desert — was slim at best.

The sun burned the light dew off the ground in minutes, anxious to torture both men and animals. By noon, the temperature had already reached about a hundred and twenty degrees. Ned could feel his back beginning to burn. He now understood why the Indians had insisted he wear long sleeves and a heavy flannel shirt. The shirt not only protected him from the sun's rays, but helped to contain moisture, trapping his sweat and allowing it to evaporate inside and act as a coolant.

Before they'd traveled ten miles, the Indian guides turned and waved. In the distance, two other Indians and a pack horse sat on the trail, watching silently. Seeing the approaching riders, they moved forward.

Jackson turned to Ned as the posse drew nearer to the waiting pair. "It's old One Snake and his grandson," he said. "They were the ones guiding Cuen and Ratzlaff."

The four Indians talked among themselves in their own language for several minutes. "What the hell's going on?" Ned shouted finally in exasperation. "Where are my deputies?"

Yellow Hair reined over to where Ned watched impatiently. "Big man and Mexican rode on to where One Snake say Saragosa waited," the Indian explained. "At top of Shiny Rock canyon. One Snake hear one shot. They not come back and old grandfather not follow. He not take us there but I know place."

"Let's get on up then!" Ned exclaimed, spurring the roan on. Two's Riding took up the lead rope of the mule the other Indians had led through the desert and the posse continued on.

It was another four hours before the men reached the mouth of Shiny Rock canyon. Creosote bushes gave way to cottontop cactus and desert holly. Even in the rocky dryness of the desert floor, life thrived. A horned lizard broke from under a stone kicked up by Ned's mount, and scampered across the hot sand, finding refuge under a holly bush. A roadrunner jumped from a brush pile at the edge of the trail, its ragged topknot upright, its tail spiked straight out behind it as it ran.

The rubble alluvial floor became a wash bed. The walls of the canyon were a brilliant display of shattered mosaic. In some distant time, the rock must have shattered and the fissures filled with molten rock of a different color. In many places the walls looked as if huge odd shaped black stones had been mortared in place by a hand far larger than man's.

Not far ahead of the riders. Mangas awoke. It wasn't hunger that gnawed at his insides, but an awareness of being stalked. He checked the bindings on the wrists and legs of the sandy-haired man and the Mexican both, then mounted and rode back into the deep canyon. He quickly found a spot where he could see far into the desert without being easily detected.

Saragosa waited without moving in the shade of a large mesquite, until the sun had crossed half the sky. Refusing to believe that his instincts could have been wrong, he decided to move on. He would have preferred to meet his pursuers in the tight confines of the steep canyon, but it was not to be. There would be another time. He mounted up.

Reining up for one last look out of the canyon to the flats beyond, he shielded his eyes from the burning sun and surveyed the desert floor far below. About two miles distant he was able to make out some movement in a mesquite patch. He spun the horse and made his way carefully along the canyon wall toward its mouth. When his horse could no longer find footing, Mangas dismounted and continued on foot.

Finding a spot where the canyon walls were steep and the boulders plentiful and loose, he waited.

As they climbed higher into the canyon, Yellow Hair motioned for Jackson and Ned to drop farther behind. The trail narrowed between the shiny canyon walls.

"Well, at least we got a little shade," Jackson said to Ned, riding behind him. Hearing a rumble, the deputy jerked upright, searching the canyon above for the source of the sound. "What's that?"

"Rock slide!" Ned screamed. The rumble quickly became a deafening roar. Almost simultaneously the two men spun their horses around, spurred them into a gallop down the slick rock canyon bottom. Before they'd ridden ten yards the rocks began to rain all around them, crashing and ricocheting off the stone walls. The terrifying roar engulfed them, drowning out the sounds of the racing horse's hoofs on the rock shelf. Bits of gravel and small stones pelted them. Then a fist-sized rock slammed into Ned's back, knocking him from his saddle. He quickly recovered, got a dislodged foot back in his stirrup and swung back up. Crouching even lower, he whipped the big horse with the tail of his reins, riding frantically for his life.

Then, almost as fast as it had begun, the rock slide was over. Cody and Jackson reined up and looked behind them. Dust hung in the air obscuring the brilliant sunlight for a moment. The canyon bottom was twenty-five feet deep in rock and debris. Neither the Indian guides nor the pack animals were anywhere to be seen.

"Jesus," Jackson muttered between great gasping breaths. "Do you suppose . . .

they're under . . . that mess?"

"I hope not," Ned said. He looked up. "I don't think that started naturally. I think our friend is up there somewhere." Jackson looked up as well, joining Cody in searching the canyon walls carefully.

They made their way slowly back to the huge rock pile now blocking the trail. Ned dismounted cautiously, sliding his .44/.40 Winchester from its scabbard.

"Jim," he ordered. "You climb that pile and check and see if Two's Riding and Yellow Hair made it. I'll cover you just in case our friend's still watching."

Jackson dismounted, then hesitated. "I'm a real good shot, Cody," he said nervously. "How about you climbing and me coverin'?"

"It's horse piss to me, Jackson," Ned replied, "one way or the other." Ned dismounted and ground-tethered the roan in the shade of the cliff. Working his way up the rock pile, he remained close to the canyon wall until he could just see over the top. Yellow Hair was atop his horse fifty yards up the canyon, pressed against its mosaic sidewall, studying its upper reaches. There was no sign of Two's Riding. Ned beckoned the Indian down with his rifle motioning him down, then sat back covering him as Yellow Hair made his way back to the blocked trail. There was no way to lead the horses over. A leg could easily plunge between the rocks, and be quickly broken. Yellow Hair dismounted and scrambled to the top where Cody crouched.

"Where's Two's Riding?" Ned asked quietly.

"He went on. Better we not be close together."

Cody nodded. "Looks like we can't get over this mess, and you can't get back. Is there a way around?"

"If there way around, Two's Riding find. We wait."

CHAPTER SIX

After having kicked the rocks loose, starting the slide, Mangas Saragosa trotted back to where he had tied his horse. Mounting, he worked his way up to a spot just above the canyon bottom, a mile above the rock slide.

Two's Riding and Yellow Hair had been leading the white eyes. They were long time enemies of Saragosa and he knew them well. They had stolen each other's horses twice, and Two's Riding had left Saragosa stranded in the desert on foot, and Mangas had returned the favor a year later. Saragosa hoped the Shoshones survived the landslide. He wanted to kill them while looking in their eyes.

As Saragosa studied the canyon, a single ride approached. Mangas levered a shell into his Henry, but let the hammer down softly and waited.

When the rider got to within fifty yards, Mangas recognized him as Two's Riding.

He carried an old Sharps resting across the saddle as he plodded slowly up the trail. When satisfied that no one else followed, Saragosa stepped out from behind the boulders and stood in the flat bottom of the wash.

Two's Riding reined up forty yards from his old enemy. Mangas stood unmoving with his legs spread, his hands holding the Henry across his thighs.

The Shoshone raised the Sharps, but gripped it by the butt with one hand. Mangas rested his thumb on the hammer of the Henry.

Two's Riding opened the mouth of the soft buckskin scabbard that hung from his wooden saddle and, carefully keeping his eyes on Saragosa the whole time, slid the rifle home. Pulling a long knife from his belt, he extended it at arm's length, the blade pointing toward the sky. Sunlight glinted off the smooth polished surface.

Accepting the unspoken challenge, Saragosa stepped to the side of the wash and leaned his Henry against the rock face. He pulled his own long-blade knife from his belt, returned to the center of the wash, and resumed his defiant stance.

The Shoshone hesitated for only a second. Then Two's Riding drove his heels into the sides of the little mustang, emitting a blood-curdling shriek as the horse leapt forward.

Saragosa steeled himself as the screaming rider bore rapidly down on him. It appeared as though the Shoshone was going to dive off the horse headfirst onto Saragosa's waiting blade. But at the last second, Two's Riding leaned backward in the saddle, threw his leg over the horse's neck, and launched himself at his adversary feet first. The move took Mangas completely by surprise. He tried to sidestep, but one of Two's Riding's moccasined feet slammed Mangas square in the chest, knocking him backward into the gravel.

Like a cat, Mangas was on his feet again almost immediately. The Shoshone bounced across the gravel, rolled over once, and stood just as quickly. The two Indians faced each other.

Mangas's tattooed body glistened with sweat as he stared at Two's Riding with burning hatred. The Shoshone stood as tall as Saragosa but was not as powerfully built.

They locked gazes for a second, then charged simultaneously. Each grasped the wrist of the other as their muscular chests collided.

As their faces came together, Two's Riding bit savagely at Saragosa's high cheekbone, catching flesh between his teeth. Mangas tore his head away, ripping his cheek in the process. Blood gushed from the wound and flowed onto his chest.

The Shoshone drove his knee upward into Saragosa's crotch, releasing his wrist while wrenching his own free. He feinted once with the knife, then kicked Saragosa in the stomach, driving him backward. Mangas stumbled over a boulder and fell heavily on his back.

The Shoshone leapt like a cougar. Diving, his flashing blade sought out the soft spot at the bottom of Saragosa's rib cage. But Mangas again caught the wrist of the Shoshone. With his superior strength he rolled over, pulling his enemy to the ground.

Mangas rolled the Shoshone onto his back and drove his blade into Two's Riding's side. At the same time, Two's Riding grabbed a handful of gravel and flung it into the snarling face of the Mojave.

With a cry, Saragosa leapt to his feet, backing away as he wiped the burning sand from his eyes.

Two's Riding clambered upright. Blood streamed from his side. He flipped his knife up, caught it by the blade, and threw it in one fluid motion toward the stumbling Saragosa. The blade sank into the knotted muscles of Saragosa's shoulder.

Two's Riding — not about to confront the powerful Saragosa with a weapon — turned and scrambled across the wash bed toward Mangas's rifle. As he raised it high, its brass receiver glittering in the sunlight, Saragosa snapped his own knife up and threw it with all his might. The flashing blade sliced through the air and caught the Shoshone in the throat.

Two's Riding gasped, dropping the Henry onto the gravel. With both hands, he reached for the bone handle protruding from his throat and tried desperately to pull the knife free. He dropped to his knees, still trying to remove the firmly embedded blade. He died in the gravel bed of the canyon, unable to curse the Mojave with his final breaths.

Mangas reached down and placed a moccasined foot in the face of the Shoshone. With one powerful tug, he jerked the blade free. Running the blade across the throat of the motionless Indian, he severed Two's Riding's neck clean through to the spine. Only then did he pull the Shoshone's knife from his own shoulder.

Mangas walked to the edge of the wash and packed his shoulder wound with mesquite leaves. Recovering his Henry and the dead Shoshone's Sharps, he climbed the canyon wall to where he'd left his horse. Saragosa mounted, then started riding silently back to his captive and prized mules.

Cody climbed back down the rubble to where Jackson stood. They loosened their horses' cinches and wet the animals' mouths with kerchiefs. Then they waited. After an hour had passed, Cody climbed back up to Yellow Hair. "You think you ought to go lookin' for Two's Riding?" Cody suggested. "Seems he's been gone a long time."

Without saying a word, the Indian climbed down to where his horse was ground-tethered. He mounted up, glancing back once at Cody. Then began to plod his way up the dry watercourse.

Cody, leaning back in the shade of an overhand, began to doze. Thoughts of home, and Mary Beth's lemonade, entered his head. He must have fallen asleep, because clattering hoofs jerked him suddenly conscious.

Yellow Hair was riding toward him leading Two's Riding's horse. Two's Riding was tied over the saddle, his arms hanging loosely.

Reaching Ned, Yellow Hair slipped easily from the saddle. Any explanation was unnecessary. The ugly wound across Two's

Riding's throat spoke for itself.

Ned looked up from the grisly sight. "Any sign of my deputies?" he asked.

"Another canyon that way," Yellow Hair said soberly, pointing to the north. "Saragosa drive mules that way. Has two more horses with iron hoofs. Track says riders on them. You go back, work around mountain. I meet you there. First I take care of Two's Riding. Water at top of Shiny Canyon no good. You watch for canyon with yellow rock. Water there. Follow track of coyote and flight of bees. They lead you."

"We'll make out," Ned said, nodding. "If we don't see you by sundown tomorrow, we'll build a big fire."

"I follow Saragosa," Yellow Hair said sternly. "He kill my friend. I kill him."

"That's fine by me, Yellow Hair. But I need to take back what's left of him. And I need to find my deputies and the mules. See you at the bottom on the north canyon." Without another word, Yellow Hair mounted, leading Two's Riding away. Ned crossed the rock fall and climbed onto his own horse, nodding toward Jackson. Together, he and Jackson began to backtrack into the desert.

Al, his wrists and ankles bound, kept his

eyes closed as his captor loaded him onto the horse and tied him to the saddle. He seriously considered letting the man know he was conscious — at least he might be able to ride upright if the man knew he was awake. Obviously, the Indian did not intend to kill him right away. Cuen couldn't help wondering why Saragosa was taking him and Ratzlaff along for the ride.

After bouncing along uncomfortably for an hour Al decided, what the hell. "Hey! You *chingaso*" he yelled at he Indian. "Untie me so I can ride right side up on this miserable horse!"

The Indian spurred his horse and rode up beside Al. They locked eyes. But it was difficult to take even Al's most ferocious look seriously with the *vaquero* hanging face down across the saddle. The Indian pulled a moccasined foot back and kicked Cuen in the ribs. Al grunted, and said no more. The Indian reined away and continued to push the mules, horses, and men forward.

They'd ridden for what Al thought must have been at least twenty-five hours. Riding belly-down tore at muscles Cuen didn't even know he had. No one was more prideful about his riding abilities than the *vaquero,* and riding like a sack of grain not only made Alvarado sore, but ashamed.

106

Finally, as the sky turned black-dark, the Indian reined up, untied the half-*reata* binding Al to the horse and flipped him off the mount head first. Al landed heavily, knocking the wind out of him. He lay gasping for air as the Indian unloaded Ratzlaff, who had yet to regain consciousness.

Lying across the fire from the big tattooed Indian, Al's empty stomach growled at him angrily. But even as hungry as he was, he did not envy the Indian who he'd watched catch, gut, roast, and devour a chuckwalla lizard. Afterward, the man had roasted and eaten a small Mojave green rattler. The fine white meat had looked tasty and smelled even better. Al's mouth, to his surprise, began to water.

A swallow of water would be welcome, he thought, but thought better of asking. The last time he had called attention to himself he had gotten a kick in the ribs for his trouble. The next time might be worse. The Indian had found a water hole and watered himself and the horses and mules, but had offered none to Al nor even bothered to wet Al's mouth or the unconscious Ratzlaff's.

Cuen knew they wouldn't last long without water. He wondered as he watched the Indian take a deep drag on his water gourd, how long would it be before his tongue started to swell.

Darkest night had taken full charge when the Indian bound them to some willows. Then Saragosa left without so much as a backward glance.

"No, Frenchy. No. I'm not going to do it." Sarah stomped her foot defiantly and put her hands on her hips. "He always goes to Callie's anyways."

"And he always comes here before he goes back out into the desert" LeConte responded. "I want him up here, in this room."

"No, Frenchy. You know what that old man smells like. I got my pride!"

"Sarah. You don't have anything that I don't want you to have. You owe me nine hundred . . . let me see." Frenchy pulled a little black tally book from his rear pants pocket. "Nine hundred seventy three dollars."

Sarah McKinne's looked softened. "Frenchy, please," she purred, "don't make me do this. That old man smells like a goat, or worse."

The Frenchman smiled smugly. "I just got a new batch in." he said. "From Charley Good Book over in Bakersfield. Came in on yesterday's train. You know that fat Chinaman gets the best. Now if you want a little smoke, Sarah, you'll do as I say."

Sarah looked hungrily at the little silver dollar-sized, glass stoppered bottle nestled in the palm of Frenchy's extended hand. She snatched at it, but Frenchy jerked it away. Again he held it out teasingly. "You want a little smoke, Sarah? *Mon Cherie?*"

Sarah licked her lips. "I . . . I do need one. Frenchy."

"Then you'll do as I ask? I'll put this one on the tab . . . If you do as I say."

"Yes. Frenchy, anything."

Frenchy dug into the bottom drawer of the tall bureau in the corner of Sarah's cramped little room, removing the opium pipe, and reaching for a blue porcelain pitcher of water on the bedside table. He filled the tank of the pipe, then carefully dropped a few seeds in the bowl, mixing it with a little tobacco. He struck a match against the wall and lit the concoction as Sarah drew in deeply. The smoke passed through the coiled pipe and bubbled through the water. By the time it reached Sarah's eager lungs it was cooled considerably. As its poison flooded her dependent blood stream, she felt her frayed nerves smoothing out. When she'd finished the pipe, long after Frenchy had left her room she was calm and ready for anything life might throw at her . . . including Polecat Pete.

Downstairs in the bar, King Hansen sat quietly involved in a game of solitaire when Frenchy walked over and sat down at his table. King looked up, expecting some snapped order or another. Instead, Frenchy pulled the cork with his teeth from the bottle of Who Hit John he had carried and poured Hansen a drink.

King's eyes lit up. "Why, thanks, Frenchy!" he said gratefully. A free drink from the saloon keeper was an unusual occurrence, to say the least.

Frenchy grinned. "Think nothing of it, my friend." They chatted amiably for a few minutes about the customers, business, the weather — all things they had never bothered to discuss before. Then Frenchy asked the question he'd come to ask in the first place. "You ever kill a man, King?" he inquired, his eyes narrowing.

The big man leaned forward, hesitating for a moment. He quickly downed the second shot of whiskey Frenchy had poured him. "Killed four men that I know of," King answered quietly. "No tellin' how many more in the war. But four I looked in the eye."

"How?" Frenchy also leaned forward, his voice dropping with sudden interest.

"First one was with a . . . a sort of knife," King said. "My Pa. The runt son-of-a-bitch used to beat me regular. He come home all whiskied up and got on me 'cause I hadn't plowed more or something. He was too damned lazy to sharpen that old plow, and I sure didn't know how. Anyways, he went to beatin' in me out in the barn and I picked up a hoof pick an' stuck him." He reached across the table, tapping a corncob-sized finger on Frenchy's pin-striped waistcoat, "right in the heart. He ran most all the way back to the house, pumping blood like a wrung-neck chicken, afore he fell." King reached out and took the liberty of pouring himself another drink. "I guess he was going after Ma for help. Anyways, Ma, the only good woman I ever knowed, fixed me a sack full of food and sent me on my way. I was fifteen. I ain't been home since."

"And the others?" Frenchy asked.

"Two fellas I was riding with." He gave Frenchy an embarrassed look. "My purse turned up missin' and I figgered it was them. Cut one's throat while he slept, and had to shoot the other when he jumped up. Found my purse a little later, down by the stream where we'd washed up." King's look hardened, "Didn't much like 'em anyhow."

"The other fella," the huge man continued, "he was a railroad guard. I was workin' with a couple of fellas holdin' up a train. Guard went for his rifle. And I had to shoot him down."

Frenchy smiled. "Then I guess you wouldn't mind makin' a few extra dollars. Even if it meant havin' to bury some old son-of-a-bitch? Quite a few extra dollars," Frenchy added for emphasis.

King stared at his employer soberly. "Not if I can keep from getting' a rope 'round my neck."

"Rope!" Frenchy scoffed. "This is my town, King! You know I wouldn't let something like that happen. Not to a good friend like you!" Frenchy smiled and slapped King on the back. He quickly poured him another drink.

"How 'bout you, Frenchy?" King asked, hunkering his massive shoulders forward and raising his bushy brows in anticipation. "You ever stick anybody with that Arkansas toothpick you carry?"

All signs of amusement suddenly left Frenchy's face. He stood up and twirled the end of his waxed mustache between his thumb and forefinger. "It is not your business," he snarled. "You get outside and see if Polecat's in town. It is the first of the month, and he's due."

King's face fell. Hurt and confused, he rose and ambled out the door to do as he was told.

Pete's first stop in Mojave was the Miners and Merchants Bank. The bank was closed so he had to rap on the door. Seeing it was Pete, a late-working teller immediately opened up. The old prospector was their biggest depositor. Pete had never let them down and this time was no exception. He deposited forty-two ounces of gold dust and amalgam, the most he'd ever brought in at one time. He kept a little over ten ounces in his pouch. At sixteen dollars per, he had deposited five hundred twelve dollars while carrying over one hundred and sixty dollars — over four months wages for most men. Leading Moses to McCrackin's livery, he tipped the boy to rub him down and give him an extra measure of oats. Then Pete headed out, ready to celebrate.

Callie opened the viewing hole in the solid plank door at the front of her establishment. She squinted at Pete through the tiny aperture carefully. "You got money, Pole-cat?"

"What you think I come for, woman?"

Pete bellowed. "Course I got money."

"Well, let me see it."

Pete's bewhiskered face turned beet red. "Consarn it, Callie," he blustered, "I been coming here ever' month for over three years! I always had enough to take good care of your ladies, and buy a round or two of whiskey besides! Now let me in."

"Soon as you show me your money, you're welcome inside."

Pete started to say what he was thinking. But then he thought better of it and pulled the pouch from under his belt. He poured a walnut-sized pile out into his open palm.

The little viewing door slammed shut. On the other side bolts slid open with a rasping grind, and the big door opened slightly. Callie stuck her head out, looked the porch and street over quickly, then opened the door just wide enough for Pete to squeeze through. "Well, don't just stand there," she snapped. "Come on in." Pete stepped through the door and Callie quickly slammed and bolted it behind him.

Pete shook his head. They sure don't call her Cautious Callie for nothing, he thought.

After carefully locking up the bank, the teller, Sam Spreckles, went across the street to Frenchy's for a well-deserved drink. Sarah sat at his table, batting her long lashes and chatting gaily for a few minutes, then walked to where the owner stood at the bar talking to some Mexican miners from Cerro Gordo.

"Frenchy, come and join us for a drink," she purred, tugging at his sleeve.

He shook her off. "Leave me be."

"You're going to want to hear this, Frenchy. It's about Polecat."

Frenchy smiled tightly. *"Oui, mon Cherie,"* he said. "I will join you."

CHAPTER SEVEN

By two in the morning, Pete had worked his way through two blondes, a brunette, and a redhead — and he hadn't yet removed his hat.

Four down and three to go, he thought, then fell contentedly asleep in the bed of the redhead, an Irish girl with an especially sensitive nose, who escaped to a neighboring room to avoid Polecat's stench. He slept until the first light of dawn. Then he awoke, dressed and walked to the livery where he'd left his pack. He dug out two containers, then hurried back to Callie's. On his way, Pete passed the huge, pig-eyed man they called King, and for the first time in a year, Frenchy's goon tipped his hat. Pete returned the acknowledgement. It must be my reputation with the ladies, he thought smugly. Or maybe he knows I'm the only man in town who can afford to drink the Napoleon brandy his boss holds so dear.

By nine-thirty, when the first of the girls was beginning to rise, Pete already had the coffee boiled and four dozen of the lightest, tastiest, sour dough biscuits a body could ever hope to eat steaming on a platter on the parlor room table — with one tin of sage honey and one of butter waiting for good measure. The girls would need their strength. Pete knew he'd need his too.

For the rest of that day, Pete wandered from room to room until he had sampled the charms of each soiled dove. For the thousandth time, he offered Callie a miner's month's wages to allow him into her room. She refused for the thousandth time, so he offered her a hundred dollars. Even Callie seemed taken aback by such a huge sum. But with one whiff her resolve strengthened, and she refused once more.

Thinking Callie a cautious fool, Pete collected his things and headed to Elroy's Livery to pick up Moses. He tipped two bits, which elicited a broad grin and a loud "Thank you, Mr. Polecat" from the stable boy. Pete wandered out to Mojave's main street just as the sun was dipping below the horizon.

Pete needed to buy some supplies, but the general store was locked up tight by the time he got there. Now he would have to spend another night in Mojave. He'd hoped to have his drinks, give Frenchy the bad time he'd carefully planned, then make his way through the desert in the cool of night by the light of the waning moon while still feeling the numbing buzz of the Who Hit John and the Emperor's Tears. Now he'd have to leave in the heat of day after he'd provisioned up. Pete grunted in annoyance. He wasn't a man to tarry unless there was something that needed tending.

He led Moses to the rail of the Silver Gunsight and left him standing untethered. "Don't you wander off now, Moses," he ordered sternly. "I'll have one drink, then we'll go to Frenchy's and get you a taste of the frog's pride and joy." Cackling and slapping his thin, sinewy, canvas-breeched thigh, Pete banged through the doors of the saloon.

It was black as Satan's eyes by the time he stumbled back out. The waning moon had not yet risen. The prospector scratched his patient jackass's long ears and led him down the street. Pete had already had four three-finger drinks of Who Hit John before coming out to find the little burro. He imagined Moses to be eying him critically. Oh, what the hell, the old prospector thought. He couldn't leave Mojave until he provisioned up in the morning anyway.

The noise from the busy saloon permeated the still air outside. Pete cackled loudly, and dragged the reluctant Moses up the board stairs and through the swinging doors of the saloon. Once clattering inside. Moses set his legs down stubbornly and emitted a loud, reverberating bray that echoed throughout the saloon. The busy place silenced abruptly as the crowd turned to eye to old man and his squalling burro. Pete laughed, slapping his thighs while doing a little jig. Soon the rest of the crowd was roaring with laughter.

The fat bartender, Tucker Parks, stomped out from behind the bar, and King Hansen hurried from a faro table, both intent on throwing the old fool and his animal out into the street.

Pete jerked his ample pouch out from under his belt and waved it at the approaching bouncers. "I got six ounces of pure gold here," he announced. "And that's . . ."

He didn't get any further as King grabbed him by the collar and the seat of the pants and swept him off his feet. Lifting the prospector into the air, King aimed him toward the swinging doors.

"No!" Sarah screamed. "No, King." The big man turned. Pete hung, kicking and complaining, from his powerful ham-sized hands. "Put him down, King," Sarah said quietly. "Mr. LeConte says Mr. Polecat Pete is welcome here anytime."

"He didn't say nothin' about no damned cattawallin' critter, did he?" Tucker asked, tugging determinedly at the burro's rope headstall. Just as King set Pete down, the little burro pulled loose from the bartender, spun around and kicked out with his hind legs. The sharp hoofs caught the fat bartender square on the backside, knocking the man sprawling across the floor.

Tucker leapt to his feet. Fire burned in his eyes as he raced behind the bar and came up with a shotgun. Cocking both barrels, he leveled it at the braying burro. His eyes wide with fear, Pete jumped in front of Moses and spread his arms protectively. The entire room fell silent.

Frenchy LeConte stepped out onto the interior balcony that overlooked the saloon floor. "Tucker," he shouted with authority, "put the scattergun away!" Every man in the room looked up as Frenchy made for the stairway.

Taking the stairs two at a time, he hit the floor and bounded across the room. He laid his hand gently on Pete's shoulder. "Polecat, why don't you take your animal outside, and I'll buy you a drink."

King, Tucker, Sarah, and the crowd were astonished. They'd never seen Frenchy be civil to Pete, much less offer a free drink.

"Believe Moses would like a drink too, Frenchy," Pete said, his eyes sparking with new mischief.

Frenchy's eyes grew suddenly cold. "Livery's down the road, Polecat." The stinkin' old man's pushing his luck, he thought. But Frenchy kept smiling.

"Well, how 'bout you buying me one an' I'll pay for a shot or two of the Emperor's Tears for my little friend?" Pete asked. Then he guffawed loudly.

Frenchy could feel the heat rise on the back of his neck. In his mind he kept repeating, New Orleans, New Orleans, New Orleans.

"Sure, Polecat," Frenchy said, smiling broadly. He twirled his waxed mustache between his thumb and forefinger. "Why not?"

The crowd watched in amazement as a cackling Polecat led the braying burro up to the bar. Pete dug into the burro's almost empty pack and fished out a burlap sack. He turned to one of the town's drunks who leaned on the bar, drinkless. "I'll be buyin' you a bottle of Black Widow for that hat," he offered.

The drunk's eyes lit up. "Why sure, Polecat!" he said, whipping the battered hat from his head and handing it to Pete. The prospector filled it with oats from the sack and sat it on the bar, slapping the counter soundly with the flat of his palm. "A bottle of the Emperor's best!" he cried.

The big bartender, the fire still blazing in his eyes, looked questioningly at Frenchy. The saloon owner nodded affirmatively. The bartender looked crushed. He had hoped his boss would come to his senses and allow him to throw the smelly desert rat and his critter out into the street. He upended a small barrel and reluctantly climbed up on it to reach the top shelf on the wall behind the bar. Stretching as far as he was able, he just managed to reach the long-necked black bottle resting there. He climbed down and handed it to Pete, uttering an audible snarl.

"Thank'ee," Pete said grinning. He pulled the cork out with his teeth, and poured half the bottle into the upturned hat.

"Here you are my little darlin'," Pete cooed, setting the hat on the floor in front of Moses. The little burro looked at him with large, trusting eyes as Pete poured a generous dollop in his own glass. The prospector turned, and touched the glass to Moses's nose. "To the Emperor," he toasted, then killed the shot in a gulp. "Whew," Pete gasped, "that's fine as dew on a mouse ear!"

The saloon, which had been silent, now shook as the patrons roared with laughter, seeing the burro sink his muzzle into the hat and began munching and slurping away.

"That'll be twenty dollars," growled the bartender.

"Seventeen dollars and fifty cents." Pete slapped the poke of gold on the bar. "Frenchy said he'd buy me one."

Again the man looked pleadingly at his boss, and again was disappointed by Frenchy's affirmative nod. Leaning his belly on the bar, Tucker growled at Pete, "Plus six bits for the bottle of Black Widow."

Pete poured two ounces of dust onto the small scale the big man sat on the bar. "Buy everyone in the house a drink!" Pete shouted, then added quickly, "Beer or whiskey. Moses and I'll be keeping the bottle of the Emperor's Tears." Again he cackled loudly, the sound sending a chill up the big bartender's spine. The man's jaw knotted, his eyes twitched, and he gritted his teeth. He began unconsciously rubbing the stub of his ear as he eyed Pete coldly.

Pete took a towel from the underside of

the bar, lifted Moses's muzzle and wipe it clean. "There you are, Darling," he cooed lovingly. "Now try an' not be so messy."

Once again the saloon erupted in gales of laughter. The big bartender turned red in the face and stomped away.

A half-bottle later, Pete sat at the faro table against the wall, observing the game with bleary eyes. For a hopeful moment Frenchy had thought that Pete might join in. But the old prospector seemed content to just watch, sipping from the bottle of Napoleon brandy while casting hungry glances toward Sarah as she flitted from table to table. Finally, Frenchy pulled her aside, whispered something in her ear, then walked to the faro table.

"Polecat." Frenchy said in his most charming, over-embellished accent, "come to zee table in zee corner and join Frenchy for a drink."

"Why sure, Frenchy." Pete had been tiring of the game anyway. Plus Sarah had been sitting down at Frenchy's table off and on during the evening. With a little luck she'd be joining them again. Pete had long admired the beautiful, long-legged bar girl. He presumed she was a sporting woman, but had never partaken of her charms. He'd always been reluctant to approach any woman who wasn't a full time resident of a sporting house.

Pete rose wobbly, collected himself, and stumbled over to the table. He'd taken Moses outside hours ago, after the burro had expressed his disdain for the whole affair by depositing a load of well-processed desert sage on the floor in front of the bar. Had jobs not been so scarce in Mojave, Frenchy would have been in the market for a new bartender shortly after ordering Tucker to clean it up. As it was, all he had to do was put up with one shout of "I ain't no goddern nursemaid to no lop-eared, splay-legged excuse for an overgrown goat!"

Almost the instant Pete sat down at Frenchy's table, Sarah hurried over and plopped herself down between them. She had one drink, laughed and flirted shamelessly with the older man. Then, just as it appeared that Pete was getting up the courage to proposition her, she got up and left.

Frenchy was about to follow after to chastise her, when Pete reached across the table, laying his hand on the saloon owner's arm.

"That's 'bout the most beautiful woman I ever laid these old eyes on, Frenchy," Pete said breathlessly, motioning him closer. Frenchy smiled tightly, held his breath, and leaned over.

"I don't suppose," Pete whispered, "that she . . . that she is . . ."

Frenchy nodded. *"Mais oui,"* he assisted. "She is zee lady of zee house."

"A sportin' woman?" Pete exclaimed, grinning broadly.

"A sporting woman." Frenchy leaned forward, whispering into the prospector's ear. "And you are correct my friend. She is zee most beautiful woman I 'av ever seen. And I am a connoisseur of fine horses and women." Frenchy's eyes gleamed mischievously. "She will not bed just anyone, though," he cautioned.

Pete looked crushed. "Do you think . . . you think I might have a chance?"

Frenchy smiled. "You might my friend. If the stars are right and the moon is waxing and near full."

Pete's mouth fell open. "Well dang me if it ain't!" he exclaimed.

"If you are so fortunate, my friend," Frenchy said, smiling so tightly his waxed mustache quivered. "I will tell you, her skin is white and smooth as cream. And when she makes love," Frenchy paused for emphasis, "it is like zee mare munching zee oats."

"Oh!" Pete stared wide-eyed as Sarah made her way around the bar from table to

126

table. "Like zee mare," he muttered to himself, unconsciously imitating Frenchy's accent, "munching zee oats."

CHAPTER EIGHT

Having ridded himself of his old enemy, Two's Riding, Mangas drove the stock and his captives down the canyon, stopping only occasionally to eye his back trail. There was nothing. Perhaps when others found the dead man, they would turn back. He was seldom able to see more than a quarter of a mile up the twisting, turning dry water course, and sometimes much less. But the horses and mules had a much finer tuned sense of hearing and smell. They'd detect another animal, even in the deepening shadows of late evening with the hot wind blowing down the canyon.

The jenny mule had taken control of the herd and was particularly alert. Mangas watched her closely. He drove the animals into the shade of a bank and sat quietly, hearing only the sounds of the mules swishing their tails. As Saragosa readied himself for the last long drive out of the canyon and onto the desert floor, the lead jenny's ears straightened. She stood stone still, then began braying loudly.

Mangas dismounted and walked to the mules laden with the two captives. He checked the ropes. Once satisfied that they were securely tied, Mangas remounted. He drove the mules and horses into a canter, knowing that they would stop to graze in a flat with a small seep up ahead where the canyon divided into two smaller ravines.

Spinning his desert-wise mare, he began to backtrack carefully.

Several minutes later, the mare snorted and stamped, sensing another animal. Mangas pulled the horse to a stop and dismounted. Removing his Henry from its leather sheath, he slapped the mare on the flank and sent her, rope reins dragging, racing back down into the canyon. He knew she wouldn't go far.

Sinking into the shadows of a steep side wash, he waited for those who followed.

He didn't have to wait long.

Mangas heard the animals before he saw them. He levered a shell into the chamber, then lowered the hammer softly. The two approaching horses rounded a bend in the canyon floor. Saragosa could see one rider tied across the saddle. The lone surviving rider, Yellow Hair, was the only threat.

Saragosa emerged from the shadows and stood in the center of the wash, the Henry resting comfortably in his hands. Yellow Hair drew rein two hundred yards away and sat in the saddle checking the canyon walls. Convinced the Mojave was alone, he dropped the lead rope, releasing the trailing horse and its dead rider. Yellow Hair pulled his own rifle from its scabbard. With an eardrum-piercing scream that echoed throughout the canyon, he whipped his horse into a gallop.

One hundred yards from his adversary, racing at full gallop, the Shoshone dropped the reins and brought his rifle to his shoulder. The crack of his shot echoed. Mangas felt the slap of wind as the bullet cut through the air by his left cheek. Still he did not move. With his Henry held comfortably across his knotted thighs, he waited.

Another Shoshone, he thought, has come to die.

At fifty yards, the charging Shoshone levered in another shell. Yellow Hair brought the rifle butt up to his shoulder.

As Yellow Hair fired, Mangas dropped to one knee. The air above him sang as the Shoshone's bullet whizzed by.

At forty yards, Mangas raised his rifle and

fired. The Henry bucked in his hands, spitting flame and smoke.

Catching the slug square in his chest, the Shoshone's arms flung outward. The .44/.40 flew up into the air, then clattered to the rocks lining the sand wash. Yellow Hair was jerked off the back of his horse as if roped, and landed heavily in the sand. Lying on his back, he pawed at the old Colt he carried. He was dead before it cleared its scuffed holster.

Mangas walked slowly forward until he reached his kill. The small entrance wound in the man's chest looked deceptively insignificant. Hooking a moccasined-toe under the body, Saragosa rolled him over on his stomach. A fist-sized chunk had been blown out of the man's back. The flies were already gathering when Mangas knelt, pulling a handsome bone-handled knife from the Shoshone's belt, and cut the man's medicine bag from his neck. Saragosa tossed the bag into the brush. Then he scalped the man with his own blade.

The Shoshone's good medicine had run out. Noticing his own shoulder wound beginning to weep, Mangas packed it once more. He carefully selected a bud of peyote from his medicine bag and popped it into his mouth. As he chewed, he was able to forget the pain, which had receded into a deep dull ache. His vision had begun to blur from the swelling in his face. He scrubbed the bit on his cheek with clean sand from the bottom of the wash.

Saragosa caught up with the dead man's horse. Mounting up, he considered riding up the canyon to retrieve the other horse with the first dead Shoshone on its back. No, he decided. He already had more than enough livestock to handle in this desert. Turning, he whipped the little mare into a steady lope.

The mules were grazing where he'd expected them to be, with the white eyes and the Mexican still securely tied across their saddles. He looked down the left fork of the canyon. For a moment he considered taking it, it being closer to the sacred mountain. But the water was better along the right fork. And he had twenty-four head to worry about.

In two days of hard riding he would be at the sacred mountain. Then he could resupply and rest before starting the long drive to the Colorado. There he would find miners who would buy the mules. But before he left the Colorado, he would offer the Mexican to the gods — after making him sweat and squirm watching his big friend die.

■ ■ ■ ■

By the time the sound reached Cody's camp, the shots had become muffled, sourceless echoes. He considered starting up into the canyon in the failing light, but thought of his old friend Henry Hammer and what he would do. Cody decided to be patient and not give his adversary the advantage. Still, he couldn't help being worried about Yellow Hair.

Cody stretched his whipcord frame in front of the fire, careful not to stare too intently into the flames. Long ago, when he'd been working cattle with the black Indian fighter, Henry Hammer, he had been taught that gazing into campfires impaired one's night vision. It was a lesson well-learned, and only one of the many Henry had taught him when Cody was just a 'pilgrim pup', as Henry had called him.

Every time Cody came to the desert side of the Sierra Mountains, he couldn't help but think about Henry. Ned had helped Henry out of a tight spot on the first day they'd met, and Henry had returned the favor by getting him a job and teaching him how to keep it. Henry Hammer worked the Lazy Z ranch which ran cattle from Independence, in California's Long Valley, all the way to Reno. It was hundreds of miles of rugged, windblown country inhabited by both friendly and hostile red men — and you seldom knew which was which. Ned wished Henry was with him now.

Ned stood and stretched. Big Jim Jackson lay opposite the fire, poking at it lazily with a stick. Its embers sparked and rose angrily in the cold night air. The stars shone brilliantly. The moon was late in rising.

If it wasn't for all the blood that had already been soaked up by the desert floor, Cody might have enjoyed this foray, at least the night time portion of the trip. The arid, hot desert days were unbearable. All animal life hid in the shade, leaving only if any immediate opportunity arose to tempt their palate, or if they themselves were about to become something's meal.

But at night, the desert came alive.

Coyotes cried and yipped at the silver moon while owls hooted mournfully at scampering kangaroo rats and white-footed mice. Those same mice would often whistle so sharply that it would send chills up a man's back and make his teeth ache. A bobcat, successful in its hunt, screeched triumphantly as his rabbit victim wailed its last.

As Ned walked into a creosote patch to relieve himself, Mexican ground crickets scattered noisily in front of him, filling the air with their chirping chatter. Ned kicked a tall creosote in passing and a hundred Bruner's silver-spotted grasshoppers gave up their roosting place. Their wings and green-mottled bodies flashed in the fire light as they fled to another creosote.

At night, the temperature dropped sixty degrees; halving itself from the one hundred twenty it had been earlier in the day. The air — malevolent in its dryness even though remarkably cool — whispered through screw bean mesquite and rattled desert holly.

And all the night sounds paid homage to the stars.

Ned pulled his bedroll away from the fire, deciding it was time to climb between his thin blankets. He had no wish to be highlighted by the fire's dim glow — for the lower animals and reptiles might not be the only night hunters out this night.

If Mangas Saragosa knew they followed — and Cody was positive now he did — he, too, might wish to take advantage of the darkness.

Cody bit a knuckle, furrowed his brow, and wondered if they'd actually made any real progress. They'd found the shallow, yellow-rocked canyon and the muddy, scum-covered water it held. Though rank tasting, they hadn't sickened from drinking it and the horses seemed strong and sound after slurping up their fill. Yellow Hair had not made an appearance at the appointed meeting place near the mouth of the north canyon, where they now camped.

That fact, and the cracking gun shots that had reverberated down the canyon in the last light of day, made Cody cautious. He tried to find the constellations he'd memorized as a boy, to keep his mind off the manhunt he had to continue in the morning.

Unless there was another exit from the canyon. Saragosa was still up there somewhere.

If Ned had known the country, he could have gone on at night. With the late rising, three-quarter moon, he decided it would be possible to leave well before first light. Saragosa traveled with captives, if Yellow Hair had read the sign correctly. Cody hoped it was his friends. And that they were still alive.

Ned threw back the blankets, unable to sleep. He dug a pipe and pouch of tobacco from his bedroll. Smoking was a habit he'd picked up from Hiram Nelson, the former city marshal of Bakersfield and Cody's mentor and friend. Ned sat on his bedroll and packed the pipe tightly. Then he rose and walked over to the fire. Finding a dry twig, he stuck it in the flame, then used the ignited end to light up. Then Cody walked into the desert. A sandstone outcropping at the mouth of the canyon invited him to sit, so he did. He smoked quietly, listening to the night sounds, and thinking.

Jackson coughed in his sleep and rolled over closer to the embers of the dying fire.

Ned eyed the sleeping Jackson. Again the sheriff silently wished Henry Hammer was with him. Unlike Hammer, Jackson had flapped his jaw continually right up to the time when Ned informed him of Two's Riding's fate. Big Jim had paled, and then fell strangely silent. He hadn't said ten words since. Ned was developing the uncomfortable feeling that, as big and formidable as Jackson was, he would cut and run at the first sign of trouble.

Cody sighed. If only his partner was Henry Hammer, or Theo Ratzlaff, or Alvarado Cuen, or even old Hiram Nelson. Anybody but Jim Jackson.

But even more than that, Cody hoped those two iron shod horses that Yellow Hair said ran with Saragosa weren't carrying *dead* weight.

Theo Ratzlaff moaned and opened his eyes.

Cuen heard the sound and turned his head. He could see enough in the rising moon to know his big friend had come to.

"You're going to be all right, Theo?" Cuen whispered.

"Where the hell are we?" Ratzlaff asked, then mumbled, "Son-of-a-bitch," as he struggled at his bound wrists and ankles.

"You're correct there, *amigo,*" Cuen said. "It's a son-of-a-bitch who has us. We're guests of Mangas Saragosa."

"We got any water?" Theo rasped through parched lips.

Cuen shook his head. "He hasn't given us any all day. He watered the horses and mules, and filled his own tattooed belly."

Theo lay quiet for a moment, then winced as he rolled over on his back. "Son-of-a-bitch!"

"Are you calling me, *amigo*?" Al asked. "Or complaining about that split in your *cabezo.* It's a good thing we hit your hard Russian head. Anywhere else it would have killed you."

"Very funny, Chili pepper." Theo glanced around the camp. "Where is the dog eater?"

"I don't know," Al answered. "He left

camp, if you can call this piss hole a camp, about an hour ago."

"My head feels about the size of a pumpkin," Theo complained, "and I'm seein' two of you." He closed his eyes and lay back, wincing once again. "And one of you is ugly enough to make the hair fall off a hog."

Al smiled tightly. "That's a good sign," he said. "As long as you're complaining and pitching insults, you can't be hurt too bad."

"Couldn't prove it by the way I feel." Theo raised his head slightly and squinted, trying to bring his eyes into focus. "You think Ned is trackin' us?" he asked.

Cuen sighed. "I hope so, *amigo.* I truly hope so."

Alvarado noticed the Indian had dropped their saddles twenty feet from where they lay. On the back of each were tied the leather water bags.

"Theo," Cuen asked breathlessly. "You think you can wiggle over to those saddles? With a little luck, we could pull the stoppers with our teeth."

"You bet your bean-brown butt, Chili pepper."

Grunting and wincing with pain, they both wiggled and squirmed slowly across the ground. They regularly had to stop and back up to extricate themselves from mesquite bushes and to avoid small boulders they couldn't cross. But after what seemed like an agonizing eternity, they reached the saddles. They worked their way into position, grunting and puffing. They grabbed the stoppers with their teeth, pulled, then greedily drank their fill.

Al could feel the strength flowing back into his body as the water flowed down his parched throat.

Getting the stoppers out was one thing, getting them back in was another altogether. Most of the remaining water spilled from the bags in the process, disappearing into the sand. But Cuen and Theo would last another day.

They wiggled back to the spot where Mangas had left them just moments before the big Mojave returned to camp. Saragosa stared at them thoughtfully, noticing the tracks their effort had made in the sand. He crossed to the water bags, pulled the plugs loose and squeezed the last drops of liquid onto the sand.

"Dog eatin' nigger," Ratzlaff mumbled.

Mangas rose after emptying the bags and walked over to the prostrate Ratzlaff. He muttered something unintelligible, then kicked Theo in the stomach.

Theo uttered a pained "umph". His eyes

burned with cold fire as he glared at the tattooed Indian. But he said nothing.

Saragosa walked over to Alvarado, who tried vainly to roll out of the way, and kicked him heavily in the ribs. Then the Indian walked off into the darkness.

Cuen and Ratzlaff lay panting in the dust.

Sarah sashayed over to Frenchy's table. She spun the spindle-backed chair around and sat backward in it facing Polecat. Her long, net-stockinged legs extended out from under her pushed up satin skirt to rest on either side of Polecat's canvas-breeched, quivering legs. Pete had been watching her for so long, and thinking about Frenchy's intimate comments, that her proximity nearly made him faint.

Winky, the piano player, banged away his own off-key version of "Buffalo Gal" on the upright. Sarah tapped her heels in time, her breasts jiggling seductively.

"You want to buy a thirsty girl a drink?" Sarah asked, winking dark eyelashes at the old man.

"Excuse me," Frenchy said, jumping up from the table. "I got business to attend to."

He's drooling in his whiskers, Sarah thought, with a slight shudder as she smiled at the prospector. But Frenchy had made it very, very clear. No Polecat Pete in her room meant no more heavenly delight in the pipe. If she could only get out of this town and on to San Francisco, things would be different. Long ago, when her train had stopped over briefly in Mojave, her money had been stolen. Since then she'd come to suspect it had been Frenchy or one of his flunkies who'd done the deed. The money had been stashed in her carpet bag which had been left on a bench while she checked with the station master to see when the train would be moving on. But without money *she* couldn't move on. She needed a job, and Frenchy LeConte had the only one in town. Sarah had never worked before. The man she'd lived with in Galveston had gotten the consumption. If Sarah hadn't been clever enough to hide a little money away each time she sold something of his to keep him in drink, she'd have never even gotten this far. She'd lived in sin with the Galveston man — though they'd told everyone they were married — but she'd never been anything quite as sinful as a sporting woman.

Then Frenchy introduced her to the heavenly delights and, before long, she *had* to have it. Frenchy had promised her she'd never be expected to sell herself. At first it was just a drink or two with the customers. Then it was drink with the customers and sleep with Frenchy. Then, as the opium took more and more control, it was sleep with any men who had the money, and give all the money to Frenchy.

Now all she wanted out of life was smoke — and the chance to go on to San Francisco to get away from Frenchy. She'd heard that there were opium dens on every corner in San Francisco.

She turned her thoughts back to the old man who leaned across the table drunkenly. "I'll buy you the whole dang bottle," Pete slurred.

"Why, that's sweet of you Polecat," Sarah whispered, batting her lashes. "You got enough left in that pouch of yours?"

"I got enough, little lady, an' plenty more where that came from." Pete looked around to make sure no one could overhear. Then he whispered, "How about . . . What do you say we . . . Oh, consarn it woman, let's you an' I take a bottle up to your room." He wanted to cut his eyes away from her jiggling breasts but he was hypnotized.

Sarah smiled knowingly. "Why, Polecat," she purred. "Just how much gold do you have left in that pouch?"

He pulled the small bag from under his

belt and weighed it in the palm of his hand. "I bet there's the better part of three ounces here, little lady," he said.

"I hear you pay double at Callie's, Polecat." She smiled gaily and Polecat blushed. "And that's not double around here."

Pete flushed. Two dollars was double at Callie's. He stood up to leave but she grabbed his arm. "But then, I always have been partial to older men," she added. She rose and walked toward the stairway, glancing back over her shoulder coquettishly.

Polecat smiled broadly, displaying his tobacco-stained teeth, and followed Sarah as faithfully as his little burro followed him.

As soon as Pete and Sarah had crested the top of the stairs and disappeared down the hall, Frenchy waived King over. "Close it down, King," he ordered brusquely. "I want everybody out in five minutes."

"But boss, it isn't even midnight yet!" His boss's cold, hard look effectively killed any further objections and King turned to inform the customers that it was lights out in five.

Polecat Pete was already stripped to his long-johns when Sarah propped a foot up on a chair to roll down a garter and net stocking. Pete sat eagerly on the edge of the bed. The corn shuck mattress crackled and bounced slightly as he watched the beautiful woman undressing. Her legs were as smooth and white as the cream Pete had churned for his mother fifty years earlier.

Once she had gotten both stockings off, Sarah reached behind her and began unbuttoning her satin gown. Pete sucked in a deep breath as her straining breasts sprang free of their constraints.

Suddenly the door burst open with a crash. King Hansen charged into the room followed by Frenchy LeConte. Sarah screamed. Before Pete could rise, the huge, pig-eyed King was on him.

The big man jerked Pete's arms behind him and shoved the old man's face into the mattress to muffle his yelling.

"Hand me those," King growled at Sarah, holding Pete's wrists behind him with one massive hand. He reached out and snatched the stockings out of Sarah's grasp.

She stormed toward them. "What in God's name are you doing?" she demanded angrily.

"You stay out of this, *Cherie*," Frenchy warned.

Pete twisted his face away from the mattress. "You ain't gettin' my gold mine, you frog-eyed excuse — !" he managed to scream before King's ham-like fist knocked him senseless.

"Don't kill him, imbecile," Frenchy snapped as King bound Pete's wrists tightly with Sarah's net stockings.

King looked up, his small eyes reflecting his pain. But he said nothing.

"You *do* want his gold mine!" Sarah said angrily. The fear on her face had suddenly turned to steely determination. "I got him here, Frenchy. I want my cut."

Frenchy jerked his Arkansas toothpick from its sheath and shoved the needle point under Sarah's chin. She snapped her head back immediately.

"You will get a cut, *Cherie.*" Frenchy spat. "But not the kind you speak of."

In a flash, King leapt from the bedside and grabbed Frenchy's knife-wielding arm in his vise-like grip. "No, Frenchy," he said firmly. "Do what you want with this old man, but you'll not hurt my Sarah."

Both Frenchy and Sarah stared at the huge man with open-mouthed awe. As far as they were concerned, King had never even given Sarah a second glance. Blood trickled from the scratch beneath Sarah's chin. King bent Frenchy's arm backward until the saloon owner dropped the knife. It clattered noisily to the board floor. Only then did King release him.

"Sure, King," Frenchy said softly, staring in amazement at the huge man. "You know I wouldn't hurt *mon Cherie.*"

"King and I want our cuts, Frenchy," Sarah insisted. "An equal cut!"

Frenchy looked from Sarah to King then back to Sarah again. When he smiled, his waxed mustache quivered slightly. "Certainly, *mon Cherie,*" Frenchy said brightly. "Frenchy would have it no other way."

King grinned. His small eyes lit up triumphantly. He stuck a hand out to Frenchy. "Partners!" he shouted. "We're partners." Frenchy smiled back tightly as his hand disappeared, lost in King's huge palm.

"Partners," Frenchy agreed. *But for only a short while,* he thought.

CHAPTER NINE

Ned slept fitfully. Waking as the late-rising moon entered the last quarter of the night sky, he stoked up the fire, then nudged Big Jim Jackson awake. Cody shook out his boots, banged them on a rock and shook them again before pulling them on. A hidden scorpion could very easily cut this manhunt short. Retrieving his .44 from where he had laid it across a rock, Ned strapped it on tightly. He pulled his felt hat low, then turned to Jackson. "Let's bean up good. It's going to be a long day." Ned turned and started to walk back to the sandstone ledge to see how much moonlight had reached into the canyon.

"This is bullshit," Jackson mumbled, pulling on his own boots. "If those Shoshones are dead, we might as well pack it up."

Ned retraced his steps and glared coldly at his deputy.

"Why do you care about this greasy digger

Indian?" Jackson went on. "Those Harmony Borax boys offer you a big reward you didn't bother to mention to the rest of us?" The big man stood and poked a stubby finger in Ned's chest. "I'm headin' home."

Ned took a step backward, sailed his hat over to his bedroll and unbuckled his gun belt. Flipping it onto the blankets, he stepped back and looked Jackson coldly in the eyes.

"First, Jackson," Cody snarled. "I care about my people. I got, *we* got, two deputies up there somewhere and I care about doin' the job I'm paid to do." Ned raised his face until he was nose to nose with the bigger man. "You are going up that canyon with me, Jackson!" Ned insisted coldly. "If you run out on this now, I'll see you never work as a lawman again. And when I get back, I'll drag your yellow ass into the middle of the street and whip you like a stepchild . . . while telling the whole town why I'm doin' it!"

Jackson's face turned fiery red. Without warning he balled up his fist and swung it toward the sheriff. Cody ducked, avoiding the blow easily. The big man's momentum spun him completely around. Ned put a foot in the middle of his broad backside and shoved hard. Jackson lost his footing, tripped over his bedroll, and rolled into the fire. He leapt to his feet screaming, "I'm afire, Cody! Help!"

The fire had lit the fuzz on his linsey-woolsey shirt. It burned quickly, a bright blue flame.

Cody, more out of meanness than necessity, grabbed two hands full of sand and flung them over the hysterical man. Jackson dropped to the ground and rolled, screaming in terror. When he realized the danger had passed and his body had not been scorched. Jackson looked sheepishly toward Ned.

"Fix some of the sow belly," Ned growled, "and heat some beans." He turned to pick up his hat and gun belt. "I'm gonna take a look up this canyon," he said strapping on his holster.

By the time Ned returned to camp, the bacon was frying and the pan bread was browning. The two men ate in silence. Then they packed up, saddled, and started picking their way up the dark canyon.

"No, no, no, Sarah." Frenchy was adamant. "You are not going into the desert with us. Talk some sense into her, King." The big man looked away sheepishly, blinked his small eyes, and shrugged his massive shoulders. He wanted to do what pleased Sarah, but he knew the desert was no place for a woman. Sarah stood defiantly in men's pants and shirt, stubbornly insisting upon a horse to ride.

"Yes, I am going, Frenchy," Sarah said firmly, standing in the dark alley behind the saloon, blocking Frenchy's horse. King, two pack mules, Polecat Pete — bound, gagged and tied to the saddle of a Roman-nosed horse — and Moses completed the string.

It was near dawn, and Frenchy knew he had to get out of town before they were seen. "I said you are not going, *Cherie,*" he hissed. "We will bring your share back with us!" Frenchy attempted to stare down the saloon girl but he could barely make out her eyes in the darkness.

"I'll go, or I'll tell everyone in town where you've gone and what you're up to," Sarah threatened.

Frenchy sighed. This was a bad way to start a trip, being backed down by a whore. But finally he relented. "King, go to the livery and saddle my buckskin mare," he said, sighing. "You can catch up with us down the road. We will stay on it until we pass the gypsum loading ramp." King dismounted and handed the reins of his horse to Sarah. She raised one dainty foot and waited, looking into the confused pig-eyes of the big man. He smiled foolishly, finally understanding. He reached down and with one ham-like hand, boosted her into the saddle. He was still smiling as the string made its way out of the alley. It was the very first time he'd touched "his Sarah".

Pete moaned, his face black and blue and swollen. Ugly circles of scab covered his cheeks and neck and the back of his arms. It was a good thing Frenchy had emptied the saloon, because Pete's screams and curses could be heard loud and clear downstairs once Frenchy started to use the hot tip of his cigar to get the old man to talk. As much as Sarah wanted her piece of Polecat's mine, she'd had to leave the room during that part of the persuasion session.

The sound of hoof beats caused Frenchy to draw the long-barreled Remington revolver he now carried, but it turned out to be only King catching up.

A Frenchman, a giant leading two mules, a whore, and an unconscious prune of a prospector reined off the main road and headed into the desert.

Moses trotted blissfully along behind.

CHAPTER TEN

Ned was growing more and more apprehensive as he and Jackson moved deeper into the narrow canyon.

The shots that had echoed down the canyon the night before were an affirmation that someone was there and that trouble, more than likely, was there as well. Ned and Big Jim advanced a mile before the first furtive rays of sunlight appeared in the sky above. It was still dark in the depths of the canyon and its walls seemed to rise higher and higher the further they continued.

Jackson rose well behind Ned, solemn, brooding, and silent.

A roadrunner broke from a clump of desert holly almost directly beneath the hoofs of Dancer. The horse reared and back-stepped. Jackson spun his own horse around and was forty yards down the canyon before Ned called for him to stop. He lagged fifteen yards back as they continued.

The black shadows of the canyon turned to purple, then gray as the sunlight began to creep down its steep side walls.

Dancer shied again and side-stepped. Ned fought for control. The big horse's withers shivered, and he snorted his displeasure.

"What is it?" Jackson asked. He hadn't bolted this time, but had turned his horse to face down the canyon. Cody put a finger to his lips, then dismounted and tied the roan to a screw bean mesquite. Slipping the Winchester from its scabbard, Ned started up the canyon on foot. Big Jim Jackson palmed his Colt, and waited on his skittish mount.

Jackson searched the side walls of the canyon, nervously expecting the flash of a rifle blast at any moment. He flinched when he heard hoof beats clattering down on him from the rocks above. Jackson wanted to run away but dismounted instead. He tied up his horse, carried his rifle into the patch of mesquite, levered in a shell, and waited.

It was Cody, leading a pinto horse with the dead Indian, Two's Riding, tied across it.

Jackson stepped from the brush. "No sign of the other gut eater?" he asked.

"No." Dancer shied at the smell of blood and pulled against the tied lead rope.

"Whoa, Dancer. It's all right, boy," Ned said calmly as he stroked the big horse's blazed white nose.

"There's a flat up there, full of track," the sheriff continued. "Some shod and some not. Looks like they took another branch of the canyon out."

Ned untied the roan and mounted as Jackson went for his own horse. "And there's buzzards circling on up the canyon a ways." He pulled off his hat and mopped his brow with his sleeve. "Much as I hate to think what we might find, we'd better work our way up there afore we go after Saragosa and the mules."

"I'd rather be at Frenchy's," Jackson muttered, but mounted and spurred his horse up beside Ned. He had to fight to keep his mount from shying at the sight and smell of the dead Indian. Quieting the gray, he wrinkled his nose with disgust. "We better be putting' this one in the ground. He's already getting' ripe."

"Let's get on up the canyon first," Cody said. "There may be more than one to plant. I hope to God those buzzards aren't pecking at Ratzlaff and Cuen."

Ned led the pinto and its Indian burden away. Jackson waited until Cody was twenty-five yards in front before he followed.

Before they'd ridden another half-mile, they found Yellow Hair lying scalped where Saragosa had left him. The vultures had already feasted on his eyes. Ned found a strong mesquite branch and walked up out of the bottom of the wash to begin scraping a grave. "You go to collecting rocks, Jackson," he ordered. "I won't have critters getting to these men." They covered the Indians in a common shallow grave, then lined it with rocks so they couldn't be dug up.

Jackson mounted as they finished, but Ned hesitated. Standing by the grave, he removed his hat. He looked over to Big Jim. "Take that hat off!" he snapped.

"For a couple of gut eaters?"

"Take it off now, Jackson!"

Jackson smirked, but removed his hat anyway.

Cody bowed his head. "I didn't know these men well, Lord," he said, "but they were good men. They did their job and I guess that's about as good a thing as you can say about a person." He ran his hand through his mane of chestnut hair then put his hat back on his head. "Make room for 'em, Lord."

As Cody reined away, Jackson mumbled "Ain't no gut eaters in heaven. They got their own place."

Ned pushed Dancer hard. He trailed the pack mules and Two's Riding's pinto. They followed the band of horses and mules down the right hand fork of the canyon at a trot. The little seep in the flat where Cody had first picked up the trail was foul with the mess of the horses and mules and, once again, they were unable to obtain water.

After they'd ridden hard for four or five miles, the canyon began to flatten out. Cody could see far across a flat alluvial plain. At the bottom of a wide valley, two or three miles distance, was a stand of river willows and a few cottonwoods. It was a sure sign of water — hopefully more than Saragosa could foul.

The track of the band of horses and mules led straight across the plain toward the trees.

It was nearing noon. The desert shimmered with heat and false lakes as they neared the willows.

Jackson caught up to Cody. "You just gonna ride right into that thicket?" the deputy asked. "I'd bet a month's pay that Saragosa is waitin' there in the shade." He added sarcastically, "He's too smart to ride in the heat of day."

"I gotta find him to catch him," Cody said. "So we're riding right on in."

Mangas Saragosa sat on the high bank of the far side of the wash, where he could see over the willows. Silently, he watched the men approach. They were still over a mile away and he took the time to clean his Henry. The horses and mules were well-watered so he'd driven them up and around the bend to another patch of willows and some new-grown grass. The river surfaced in four spots through the valley.

The section Mangas was guarding had more water holes than he could poison. He hadn't wanted the men who followed to be able to fill their water bags. But at this place they could. He decided to kill the white men here, rather than have them chase him all the way to the sacred mountain.

The mountain was home to Mangas — and only one white man was allowed there.

The riders reined up a quarter mile on the far side of the willows.

"Cody," Jackson snarled, "I ain't riding into that stand of trees."

"You circle around and see if the mule track comes out the other side," Cody ordered. "I'll ride in from this 'un here."

"If it does, I'll be comin' in from the other

side. Don't get trigger happy."

"It won't be me who shoots you, Big Jim."

Jackson reined away and set a path that would keep him a quarter mile away from the willows. Cody rode straight toward them.

The slope was mostly low desert holly and arrowweed. Except for the willows and the cut along the sides of the wash bottom, there wasn't much of a spot for a man to hide. Still Jackson was nervous as he searched from one clump of brush to another. Once Cody disappeared into the willows, Jackson braced himself, expecting at any time to hear a rifle's report.

Big Jim came to the wash bed. He crossed where it was dry. He was greatly relieved to see the track of the mules and horses on the other side. With a deep sigh, Jackson reined his horse and started back up the dry wash bed to the willows.

Mangas crouched at the top of a ledge as the big man approached. It would be an easy hundred yard shot. At that range Mangas could pick a man's eye out.

He laid the Henry across a rock and waited.

Just as he centered the bead on the man's chest, the rock exploded in his face. He jerked backward, inadvertently squeezing off a shot. The shell kicked gravel in front of the big man's horse as Mangas levered in another shell. He looked quickly toward the willows, hoping to see who had shot at him. Seeing no one, he turned his attention back to the big man in the wash bottom. The man was fighting to keep his horse steady, trying to pull his rifle from its scabbard at the same time.

Mangas brought the Henry to his shoulder and snapped off a shot just as the man's horse reared.

The shot hit Big Jim high in the thigh, knocking him spinning from his saddle. His horse bolted, dragging him several feet before Jackson was able to shake his foot free of the stirrup. Clambering into a patch of arrowweed, he kept his face down low in the dirt.

Cody tried to get off another shot, but the Indian had disappeared. Passing through the willows, Cody had caught a brief flash of light off the Henry's brass receiver in the rocks above Jackson. Cody had fired off a quick shot, more as a warning to Jackson than anything else. The flash had been well over three hundred yards away.

Now Jackson had disappeared from sight, as had the man in the rocks. It was as if he'd never been there at all.

There was total silence. Not even the birds

and animals were stirring.

Ned began working his way out of the willows. He waited at the wash edge, carefully searching the rocks for any sign of the ambusher.

Nothing.

He ran across the wash and dove into a clump of mesquite, then continued working his way toward where the man originally been spotted.

From rock to rock, he crept. When he got to the sniper's spot, Cody could find nothing but the single ejected cartridge. He stood, then carefully climbed to the top of a boulder and searched the slope above.

There was no sign of anyone.

He heard a distant yell, and then the hoof beats of many animals. Cody gritted his teeth, wanting desperately to pursue. But his deputy was down there somewhere, probably dying — or dead.

Ned picked his way down through the rocks to where he'd last seen Jackson. Big Jim wasn't there, but a thin trail of blood indicated his direction. Ned found the deputy sitting in the brush, his belt wrapped tightly around his upper thigh, his breeches leg soaked in blood. Jackson's eyes flared with pain and fear.

"Son-of-a-bitch almost shot my balls off," he moaned.

"Let me help you on Dancer," Cody offered, "and we'll get back to the cover of the willows. Then I'll take a look."

Somehow Cody got the big man to his feet and into the saddle. Then he led the horse back to the willows and tied him up where he could reach a nearby water pool.

Ned cut Jackson's breeches leg away. There was a clean entrance and exit wound on the inside of his upper right thigh. Luckily the slug had missed the bone. Still the leg bled profusely, even with the belt wrapped tightly in place.

"Must have hit a big vein or artery," Ned mumbled as he searched his bedroll for his extra shirt. Finding it, he tore it into long strips. Making a compress, he used the strips to tie it tightly in place.

The bleeding slowed but still oozed.

"I never shoulda left Mojave," Jackson complained, wincing as he lay back in the shade of the willows.

"Well, one thing's for sure, you're not going anywhere as long as that leg's bleeding." Ned rose and started into the brush. "I'm gonna gather some wood for a fire. You try not to move."

Cody had been gone for a few minutes when another rifle shot caused Jackson to jump. The deputy shivered, certain Cody was dead and that the Indian would be walking into camp looking for him at any moment. But a minute later Cody returned carrying a rabbit in his hand. Gutting and skinning it, he had a stew well under way before the sun had cast its last lingering rays across the desolate valley.

What little sleep Cody was able to get that night, he got well away from the fire where Jackson rested. With each crackling in the brush or cry of a night animal, he found himself jerking awake. But he really didn't think the Indian would be back. With one of them wounded. Saragosa probably expected them to return to town. But Cody wasn't going anywhere, not without that Mojave lying across his saddle and the mules in front of him. Jackson was in no condition to ride, so Cody made a decision. He would make a good camp here for the wounded man and then go on alone. There was plenty of water and they could split up the food. With a hard day's ride, he should be able to catch up to a man driving over twenty head of stock easily and be back in the willow camp by the next night — with any kind of luck.

Ned shook his head. So far luck, he admitted to himself, had been riding with someone else.

CHAPTER ELEVEN

"Don't touch me with the cigar, you frog!" Polecat screamed. "I'm, tellin' you straight! Just keep on northeast and we'll be there tomorrow!"

As Sarah watched, Frenchy puffed the cigar until the tip glowed bright red. "Please don't burn him again, Frenchy," she begged. "He's telling the truth."

Frenchy mopped his brow with a kerchief. It had been white when they'd started. Now it was brown and damp. They'd ridden half the night and all day, stopping to make a dry camp when the sun disappeared behind the mountains. While Sarah did her best with beans and biscuits, King took care of the stock.

The old desert rat could have discovered a mine a little closer to Mojave, Frenchy thought bitterly. He hated the desert and the heat.

Sarah hadn't soaked the beans enough, so

they were still hard. Frenchy almost broke a tooth as he bit in. He cursed her in French, then rolled out his blanket, checked Polecat's binding, and went to bed. He was soon snoring.

Seeing Pete's wrists seeping blood from the tight hemp rope, Sarah dipped into a can of lard and spread it on his wounds to soothe them as best she could. Then she and King sat by the fire, listening to the night sounds. Pete rolled to his back and wriggled over closer to them.

"You two know that the frog won't be taking no partners in my mine," Pete said breathlessly.

"Shut up, old man," Sarah whispered. "He's got *two* partners."

"Just 'til he finds the mine," Pete insisted. "Then I wouldn't give a tinker's damn for your chances."

"Sarah said for you to shut up," King growled.

Pete switched to a different tactic. "Sarah, you never struck me as the kind of girl who's stand for an ol' man bein' mistreated," he said plaintively.

"The kinda girl I am is the whoring kind, Polecat." Sarah rose and looked pensively out into the darkness. "I guess when a body goes to whoring, she'll do about anything for money."

"Why, Sarah, whores is always been my favorite kind of woman." Pete grunted as King bent over and picked him up by the belt with one hand, then carried him a few steps away from the fire and dropped him unceremoniously.

"You stay here and keep your mouth shut, old man," he ordered. "Just like my Sarah says."

"You are as dumb as you are big!" Pete called as King walked back to the fire. "In fact, I'd call you donkey dumb if it wasn't an insult to Moses!"

King turned and gave Pete a look that shut him up immediately. Even a playful kick from that brute, Pete reasoned, could ruin a man for life.

It wasn't long before Sarah and King were asleep.

Pete waited until he was positive they were out. Then he whistled softly for Moses. The little donkey trotted to Pete's side. Pete rolled over onto his stomach. Talking to his old friend, he tried to figure out how to get the animal to chew at the hemp ropes that bound him. He pleaded with the animal and cajoled. But try as he might, Pete couldn't budge the donkey.

After more than two hours, Pete finally

fell asleep. His last thoughts were of the Emperor's Tears. If he could only soak the ropes in that good Napoleon brandy, he'd bet Moses would eat them clean through.

He knew by the stars it was almost morning when he awoke. The answer had come to him in his sleep. Sugar! Sarah had a can of sugar near the fire. If Pete could crawl to it, and somehow douse the ropes with the sweet substance, Moses would doubtlessly begin munching away.

It took the old man twenty minutes to wiggle over to the fire. It took another ten to knock the can off the rock and get the lid off. The eastern sky was glowing burnt-orange by the time Pete had rolled to his side, flipping the sugar up repeatedly with his finger until the lard sticky ropes were covered with sugar and sweetened dirt.

Again he whistled for the little burro. Pete had to wait until the burro had lapped up all the sugar in the can before he got interested in the ropes. Then the burro almost licked his writs raw before he started gnawing at the bindings. Pete grimaced but remained silent.

Pete felt the ropes loosen a little and fought to free his hands. The feeling was coming back into his fingers with stabs of needle–like pain, but the bonds still held him tightly.

"What are you doing?" King Hansen yelled as he jumped out of his bedroll. Sarah sat up groggily rubbing her eyes. The massive man was at Pete's side in four strides and kicked the burro sharply in the neck. Moses brayed loudly and bolted a few steps away. Then he turned and laid his ears flat, hee-hawing a donkey curse at the pig-eyed man.

King knelt and tugged at the ropes until he was satisfied that Pete was still tightly bound. "That damn burro almost chewed these ropes in half!"

"What?" Frenchy said, sitting up. He climbed to his feet suddenly. "What is the matter?"

"Look at this." King picked up the sugar tin and shook it. "That damn burro ate all the sugar and was chewing on the old man's ropes when I woke up. Another few minutes and the old man would have been loose."

"Ate the sugar?" Frenchy walked to were Pete lay. *"Sacreblue,"* Frenchy grumbled. "I will have no sugar for my coffee." He turned and walked back to retrieve something from his bedroll. Pete recoiled in fear as he realized the Frenchman had a long-barreled Remington revolver in his hand. Then he realized what the Frenchman had planned when the man raised the gun and extended his arm in Moses's direction.

Pete got his bound legs under him just enough for leverage and lunged at Frenchy, striking him at the knees with his shoulder. The Remington roared as Frenchy went sprawling onto the ground.

"Run Moses!" Pete screamed. "Run Darlin'!"

The roar of the revolver had been enough. Moses fled, his heels flying, kicking and jumping sagebrush and braying donkey profanities.

Frenchy got to his feet and fired two more rounds, which only encouraged the donkey's flight.

The angry Frenchman kicked Pete soundly in the ribs. Pete grunted, but wisely said nothing. Frenchy's eyes burned with rage.

They reheated beans and pan bread, packed, and rode out to the northeast soon after the sun had cleared the horizon. The sky glowed lemon yellow, predicting an extra hot day.

Moses followed behind at a safe distance.

"What the hell do you mean, you're leaving me here?" Jackson demanded angrily.

"You can't ride anyway," Ned explained.

"If you do, you'll just bust that wound open and bleed to death." Ned pulled the cinch tight on his roan. "You're lucky you didn't bleed to death last night. If I don't get hot on the trail of that Indian, we'll never catch him." Ned mounted, then spun the horse to face the reclining Jackson. "I divided the grub, and you got plenty of water. You got a pile of firewood that ought to last three days if you don't squander it. I hobbled your horse and left you a mule. If I'm not back in three days, I'd suggest you try and head for Mojave. But I'm sure I'll be back before then."

"Why, I'll be a som'bitch," Jackson muttered.

"You probably won't get an argument about that." Ned reined his horse away, snatching up the lead rope of the pack mule with the pinto tied on behind it, and rode out of camp.

He picked up the trail easily noticing where the Indian had ridden out of the rocks driving the mules ahead of him. It galled Ned to know he'd been that close to the man and possibly to his captive deputies. The tracks still indicated two shod horses.

It was Ned's intent to lope the horses until he tired one, then change mounts. That way

170

he could keep up what would be a killing pace for only one animal — providing the mules lasted. The animal was only carrying sixty pounds. Ned figured he could carry twice that much at an all day gallop. Besides, he'd nipped at Ned twice while Ned was packing him. It wouldn't hurt to work a little of the feistiness out of him.

If the animals could hold up in the heat, Ned expected to catch the Indian by midday.

By noon, Ned had already changed horses four times. Ned hadn't caught the Indian yet, but he knew he was getting close. Both he and the animals had suffered from the killing pace. They were covered with grime and sweat rolled off them in brown, muddy rivulets.

The trail followed the dry river bottom for a few miles. The occasional pothole of water made the traveling easier. But that was too good to last, and soon the trail turned away from the river bottom into a flat of rough, prickly pear cactus. The cactus thinned out as they climbed onto a lava flow, but the traveling was no less rough. For the first time, Ned had to carefully track across a hard surface. Once he lost the trail and came to a sharp cliff that dropped sixty feet to the desert below. The game would have been up had he not spotted his quarry in the distance. It gave him a certain grim satisfaction to finally see the man he'd been following for what seemed an eternity. But he was still more than three miles ahead. Cody dismounted hurriedly and dug into his pack for the telescope. The mule fought him, nipping at Cody and ducking his head until Cody was forced to kick the animal squarely in the rump. By the time Ned got to the cliff's edge, all he could see was dust. The animals had disappeared over the horizon.

"You Roman-nosed, knot-head," Ned grumbled as he replaced the telescope. "Now I still don't know if that Indian's got Ratzlaff and Cuen."

On the far horizon, directly in line with the path they traveled, a dome-shaped mountain rose from the desert floor. It, combined with the starkness of the surrounding country, sent a chill down Ned's spine. He worked his way back to the trail, following it into a cut in the cliff. Soon he was on the desert floor, traveling at an easy lope once again.

Before long, the animals began to hang their tongues and Ned was forced to slow even more. Thoughts of getting back to Bakersfield and Mary Beth — plus saving his deputies — were the only things that kept him going.

The back of his neck and the back of his hands were blistering in the merciless sun. The perspiration ran into the broken blisters and burned like the touch of hot coals.

Climbing higher, Ned stopped and rested in the scant shade of a Joshua grove. He wet the horses' and mule's mouths with a wet rag, then allowed himself just enough to swish around in his own, before he mounted and pressed on. The mule was too spent to argue this time and followed blindly.

By late afternoon, Cody saw dust rising in the distance. He figured the Indian was now less than a mile ahead. Ned's determined pushing was paying off, even if the horses — and — he were tiring badly. As the sun ducked below the horizon, Ned neared the mountain. It seemed a huge bubble dome was rising out of the desert like the top of a barrel cactus. A quarter mile from the base of the mountain, he drew rein. Ned sat and stared at it for a long moment. It must be over a mile wide, Ned reckoned, and several hundred feet tall. In places it seemed smooth as Mary Beth's shoulders, and other places rough as the lava flow he'd crossed earlier.

The horses and mule hung their heads and lolled their tongues. Ned had not found water. It would be a dry camp. He had two two-gallon leather water bags that hadn't been touched, but the horses would need most of that to get through the night. It was now or never. If he didn't find water or catch the Indian soon he would be forced to turn back. He dropped the saddles and hobbled the horses as the setting sun turned the bubble dome from dark brown to orange. Ned watched a family of ravens riding the updrafts near the cliff edge. Then he noticed a movement far up the dome's side. He dug in his pack for the "bring-'em-close". The old telescope had served Ned well in the past and did so again. High on the mountain the Indian climbed an almost sheer face. Ned shivered at the thought of following.

Ned was tempted to grab the .44/.40 and try to close enough ground to get a shot off. But a miss would tell the Indian he was being followed. There still was some slight chance that the man was unaware. Instead, Ned watched him climb higher and higher until it grew too dark to see. Sighing, Cody dropped the telescope. He took his bedroll and walked a hundred paces away from the horses. He set out his blanket in a dry, fireless camp, relishing the coolness for a while. Then he fell into a fitful sleep.

Ned awoke in the dead of night to the serenade of what he first thought were coyotes, but soon realized were timber wolves. It had been years since he'd heard the deep, vibrant howl of the wolf. The sheep men had driven them out of the Bakersfield area and the San Joaquin Valley. He wished he could build a fire, for wolves had been known to be brazen enough to come into a man's camp. But a fire was definitely out of the question.

As tired as he was, it took a long time before Ned was able to fall back asleep.

CHAPTER TWELVE

The sudden darkness surprised Alvarado as he stared straight down draped over his horse. The horses' hoofs clattered on the rock floor. The Indian halted, dismounted, and unloaded Cuen and Ratzlaff roughly. He hog tied them, then left, the soft padding sound of his moccasins disappearing into the night.

"*Madre de Dios,* where are we?" Cuen whispered weakly. Even so, his voice echoed through the cavern.

"Some kinda cave," Ratzlaff answered. His voice was hoarse and raspy. "I'm so sore from riding belly down on that nag, I don't care where we are. I'm just happy to be off that damned crow-bait. My mouth's drier than a horny toad's fart. I'm lickin' my lips with a tongue like sandpaper."

"Mine are bleeding," Cuen told him.

"I don't know why that dog eater would drag us along just watch us die of thirst."

"Maybe that's *exactly* why, my Cossack friend."

"Sorry I thought of it, Chili pepper," Ratzlaff whispered. "Real sorry."

The cavern was suddenly flooded with flickering light as Saragosa rounded a corner carrying a flaming torch. For the first time, Cuen and Ratzlaff could see where they were. The floor of the cave they lay in was smooth, but beyond, both ground and ceiling were lined with stalagmites and stalactites, casting eerie shadows against the walls. The room was larger than two good-sized barns. The horses they had ridden were inside, tied to a rope picket and grazing on a pile of swathed grass piled up in a niche. They stood within reach of a small pothole filled with water that dripped slowly from the ceiling.

Carrying two stout mesquite branches under one arm, Saragosa walked over to Cuen. He dropped one of the branches to the floor. Al flinched. At first he thought the Indian was going to bludgeon him. But instead the man ran it between Al's bound arms and his back. Though Cuen's wrists were already tied behind him, the Indian took a rawhide strip and wrapped it from one end of the mesquite to the other, binding Al's elbows as he did so. Now, even if the Mexican was able to free his hands — hands that had had no feeling for two days — his arms would still be held fast. Saragosa repeated the process with Theo. He then dragged the big man over to where a willow pole, twelve feet off the floor, was wedged between two rock faces of an offshoot tunnel. He looped a rope over the pole and fixing one end to a column formed by the meeting of stalactite and stalagmite. The other end Saragosa secured in a noose around Theo's neck. Now if Theo weakened and fell to his knees, he would strangle.

Al expected the same treatment, but it never came. Instead, he backed Al up to a tall stalagmite rising six feet up from the cave floor. Wrenching his arms painfully upward, Saragosa forced them down over the point of the limestone. If Al slipped down his arms would be pulled upward as the formation thickened closer to the bottom. Eventually they would be wrenched from their sockets.

Saragosa promptly left the chamber, carrying the torch. Once again the pitch blackness took over.

"You okay, Theo?" Al called out in the darkness.

"Hunky dory. Don't guess I'll have to die of thirst, anyway."

"Do you think Cody's behind us?" Cuen asked hopefully.

"He better be. I don't think we got much future with this dog eater."

"No, me neither," Cuen said. "His reservation must not have had a Sunday school."

"Reservation, hell," Theo snorted weakly. "This boy crawled out of this hole of a cave."

Suddenly a drop of wetness hit Al on the top of his head. He looked up as another splatted in the middle of his forehead. He threw his head farther back and caught the next drop in his parched mouth. The water tasted brackish and full of minerals. But it was wet and that was all that counted. Cuen stayed with his head back for a long time, until his neck began to cramp. But by that time he caught enough drops to be able to lick his lips and even swallow a time or two. There was no use saying anything to Theo. There was no way to get the precious water to him, and informing Ratzlaff of his own good fortune would only serve to increase the big man's suffering.

After securing the men in the big cavern, Saragosa decided to pick up the supplies that the white man should have left him. He'd let the mules water, feed and rest, then offer the Mexican to the gods at dawn.

He knew where the mules would be. He found them on the east end of the mountain, a half mile from the cave entrance.

Mangas dismounted. He pulled aside a mesquite gate that opened onto a few acres of oasis in the bottom of a box canyon on the mountain's east end, then drove the mules into it. The canyon was fed by a small stream that originated in a spring almost on the top of the dome. The spring disappeared into one of the thousand caves, reappeared, then disappeared again, only to resurface on the ledge above the grassy floor of the canyon. The canyon was only twenty-five paces across and less than two hundred long. The stream vanished into the desert floor less than a hundred paces from the canyon's mouth. But for its three hundred pace length, the stream bed and canyon bottom lay belly deep in sweet grass — a verdant island in a sea of sand and rock. Mangas had blocked the mouth of the canyon with the mesquite branches years ago. He could hold the mules there for weeks if need be.

As soon as the mules were secured, he rode to the northeast side of the mountain to the flat rock he visited each month. Three years ago, Mangas had taken a bullet in his side. It was a lucky shot from a white man whose horses Mangas had been trying to steal. The man awoke as Mangas was leading the mounts from a five wagon camp. The man shot into the night. Mangas had lost the horses before he got all the way back to the sacred mountain. And he lost consciousness as soon as he reached the mouth of the oasis canyon.

He awoke, hot with fever, but bandaged. The bullet had been removed, and a canteen of water was at his lips.

The prospector was the only man Mangas had ever allowed to see his sacred mountain and live. The old man operated a mine on the north side of the mountain, and brought Mangas supplies every month for the privilege — one box of shells for the Henry, a can of tobacco and papers, and a tin of sugar candies. They never talked, but each month without fail the supplies were there. Neither man bothered the other. Mangas agonized over allowing the old man to scar the sacred mountain. But he would have been dead had it not been for the prospector's ministrations. As long as the old miner was the only man to visit the mine, and as long as he continued to bring the precious shells for the Henry, Mangas would let him live.

Mangas knew he mined the quartz veins that had been part of the ancient mountain long before it had been covered with lava. But the scar he made was a small one. The hunt for gold was an endeavor that Mangas had no wish to take part in. The prospector grubbed out his ore, crushed it with a small hand mill, separated the gold by baking the ore over the fire and leaching it with mercury, or panned it in the stream. He repeated the process over and over again. He did this for twenty-five days without stopping. Then he rode to town and returned to start the process all over again. Mangas had decided long ago it was the life of a crazy man.

The supplies were not on the flat rock. And they were overdue. Mangas cared little about the tobacco. But he wanted the box of shells and the candy before he set out of the Colorado. He was down to a half box of ammunition. And sucking on the hard rock candy had become the one pleasure in life he allowed himself.

Mangas rode around the north side of the mountain and checked the prospector's camp. The fire pit was stone cold.

He tied the reins to the horn and slapped the mustang on the rump. Mangas knew the mustang would return to the creek and its sweet, green grass. He watched the horse for a moment, then started a climb up the mountain to another entrance to the cave, one from which he would have a good view of his back trail. He wanted to check it before it was dark. By the time Mangas had climbed to two hundred and fifty feet above the desert floor, he was able to see his pursuer in the distance.

The man was watching him through a glass.

He too must be a crazy man, Mangas thought, to follow me alone. Saragosa shook his head. He would worry about him later. It would take hours for the pursuer to find his way up the mountain. And a man carrying a torch into the cave was easy prey — if this man was indeed foolish enough to follow Mangas onto his home ground. When he came, Mangas would kill him. But first he wanted to let the Mexican watch his big friend die. At dawn Mangas would chew the holy plant, pray, kill the big man, then take the Mexican to the mountain top. Then, with the sun god watching, Saragosa would offer him up for a sacrifice.

It would assure a good trip to the Colorado.

Then he would deal with the crazy one with the glass.

■ ■ ■ ■

Pete had thought about leading Frenchy and King on a wild goose chase through the desert. But in the end he realized it would only serve to get him killed. He didn't really give a damn about the mine anyway. It was a glory hole all right, but he had enough stuck away in the bank to last him the rest of his life. But the last person he wanted to have his mine was Frenchy LeConte. The problem was, it was doubtful that Frenchy would let him live once he took control. The others probably wouldn't live either. Somehow the thought of Sarah dying — young, beautiful Sarah — was even more repugnant to Pete than thoughts of his own death. He couldn't let that happen. He had watched her growing increasingly jittery and recognized the signs — demon opium.

Pete figured their only chance was the giant Indian — Mangas Saragosa.

Years ago, when he'd first seen the Indian lying injured beside the small trickle of water, he'd considered letting him die. The man was massive, with a knotted, muscled back as wide as an ax handle, and tattoos covering most of his body. He was an ominous sight, even helpless and wounded.

After removing the bullet, Pete bandaged him, gave him water from time to time, and waited for him to either die or wake up. He awoke, staring at Pete without speaking whenever Pete brought water and food. For two days Pete didn't relax. Then at sundown on the second day, the man rose, picked up his Henry rifle, and walked into the desert without so much as a thank you or go to hell.

After he'd gone, Pete began looking closely at the quartz chunks he'd noticed in the small alluvial fan at the base of the mountain. He followed them up the ravine to their source. Somewhere up above, maybe in the mountain itself, was the main vein. He was right. He found it in a part of the mountain that differed from the rest. Most of the mountain was volcanic basalt, a bubble dome. But the dome had encompassed a smaller, much older hill, and the hill was mostly quartz. Quartz that proved to be rich in gold.

While Pete worked, the big Indian would come and sit on a ledge and watch him for hours at a time. Pete waved at him and offered him food. But the huge man never responded. He merely watched in silence. The next time Pete went to town, he bought a box of Henry shells and tobacco and candy. When he saw the Indian watching, Pete walked to a flat rock below where the man sat and left the gifts. The next day they were gone. He repeated the process every month for the next two and a half years. In that time, he only saw the Indian twice. Still, the supplies were always gone a day or two after Pete left them.

Now he hoped the big Indian would wonder what had happened to him when the supplies weren't there. It might be his only chance to live. Maybe the big Indian would want his shells enough to come looking for him.

Pete also hoped that Frenchy wouldn't hurt Sarah. She was a whore. Pete knew that. But deep down, he felt she was a good woman. Sarah probably just wanted to be rid of old Frenchy and money was the only way she'd do it. When she'd taken the trouble to soothe his wrists with the lard, Pete had decided that he might even consider taking a bath for this woman. Hell, he might even shave.

At dawn, with the mountain looming in the distance, Frenchy was already up and stirring the camp.

"You say the mine is in that upside down pot-shaped mountain?" Frenchy asked Pete for the tenth time since they'd made camp the night before.

"I told you," Pete snapped in annoyance. "That mountain's the Devil's Bowler, and the mine's on the north side. A big outcropping of quartz and a splash of diorite. Some o' that quartz is twenty-five ounces to the ton."

"Did you locate it from the float?" Frenchy asked, "or just see the outcropping?"

Pete looked at him curiously. "You been a miner, frog?"

"I had a mine," Frenchy snarled, "down on the Colorado. Years ago. But if you call me frog one more time, I will make sure there's no reason for you to visit Callie's, ever again." He pulled the Arkansas toothpick from its sheath and pricked his finger with its needle-sharp point.

"No offense, fro . . . Frenchy," Pete said quickly. He didn't mind losing the mine, but losing his manhood would leave him no reason to live.

"What was you mining?" Polecat changed the subject.

"Lead. She was the *Fleur-de-lis,*" Frenchy said proudly. "She made good money during the war and before."

King was packing while they talked and Sarah scoured the frying pan with desert sand. Her hands were shaking perceptibly.

"Is there water at your Devil's Bowler?" Frenchy asked.

"Plenty of sweet, cool water." Pete forced a smile. The faster he got them there, the faster the big Indian might solve Pete's problem for him.

Frenchy walked to the edge of camp and stared at the dome-shaped mountain as its west side faded from orange to deep purple.

"New Orleans," Frenchy mumbled.

"What?" King asked looking up from smoothing out his bedroll.

"Nothing," Frenchy snapped. "Rest well. We will have a long day tomorrow."

CHAPTER THIRTEEN

In the darkness of predawn, Mangas Saragosa stood on the highest point on the Devil's Bowler, facing the Funeral Mountains over which the sun would soon rise.

He extended his arms, ready to embrace the sun's spirit. His fingers became talons, curling out from calloused palms.

Golden feathers grew, bulging bronzed skin, then bursting forth like spring grass, splaying outward from sinewy, muscular forearms and knotted, tattooed biceps. Bulging eyes surveyed distant crevices and canyons, and even in the darkness, brought things closer with condor vision, searching for prey — and other predators.

Screeching the cry of the golden eagle, he felt himself rising, soaring, lifting on rising waves of rippling desert heat. He became a fiery ball, a white hot comet, the essence of life itself. One with the most primeval life force — the sun.

Mangas Saragosa ascended to a mystical state. Raising his voice to the dawn, he increased the tempo of his chanting. He'd removed two small buttons of peyote from his medicine bag, and chewed them as he climbed to the edge of the precipice over-looking what the white man called the valley of death. The peyote heightened his senses, brought him closer to the Great Spirit that was the sun, and made him one with the other desert creatures. He was floating, rising to meet the fiery orb that made the desert what it was. But it had not yet appeared over the distant horizon.

Ignoring the cold desert wind on his naked torso, Mangas leaned out over the precipice with the confidence of a hovering kestrel. The last of the stars had disappeared as the night surrendered herself to day. The temperature would soon be sweltering. The clear view of the distant back-lighted Funeral Mountains would soon be dancing in macabre contortions caused by the heat waves.

He prayed for the pain in his face, now swollen and distorted and covered with the yellow mud of the rotten-egg spring, to go away. He prayed for his shoulder to heal and stop its deep ache and constant weeping.

He knew the man he'd seen last night still followed. But he also knew the man who followed could not soar to the heights were Mangas stood. He could not climb the sheer cliffs of the sacred mountain, at least not in the predawn night. Even Saragosa would have had trouble doing that.

Saragosa raised his muscled, tattooed arms. Extending them their full length, he continued to chant in a deep reverberating resonance which carried out over the black and red basalt cliffs of the ancient bubble dome and down to the desolate desert floor three hundred feet below. The wounded shoulder shot searing pain through him, but his peyote-numbed nervous system paid it no heed.

Cody had set out for the mountain two hours before sunrise.

The two gallon leather water bag hanging from his shoulder flapped against his chafed side.

You must be out of your mind, Ned thought. You could have gone back to Mojave and wired the sheriff in Lone Pine. Ned knew he was now well into Inyo County and out of his own jurisdiction. He also knew that he would follow this man to hell and back. It was now more personal than the law. The man had killed Cody's Indian guides. And, probably by now, his deputies.

The sun lingered below the horizon. The gray light of predawn defined the line of distant granite peaks. It wouldn't reach the north face of the basalt dome for another two hours. By that time, the night chill would be replaced by the hot winds racing into the valley from the Panamint Mountains, displacing even hotter air rising from the desert floor.

But now it was cold.

The wind whipped at Cody, and moaned its displeasure. He'd left creosote and screw bean mesquite bushes far below him. Now the only handholds for his cracked and bleeding hands were jagged rocks and fissures, and the smooth basalt offered few of those. But he looked around and found another. He wedged his hand in for a pull upward that would allow him to lean his chest on the ledge above and rest.

He dragged himself painfully upward. With a heavy sigh, he rested motionless until he caught his breath. Then he raised his head.

Cody found himself staring into the vertical, golden eye slots of a Mojave green rattler.

Instinctively, he flung himself backward.

His left hand remained wedged in the rock and he hung, swinging, suspended above the next ledge which was twenty feet below him. The Winchester slung across his back clattered against the rock face.

Ned cursed himself. The snake hadn't rattled, nor even moved, obviously lethargic with the cold. But the thought of being struck in the face terrified him.

He swung his body back and forth until he could regain his grip. Trying to find an alternate route would cost him too much time. And by then, the next snake might be warmed up and waiting for him. He worked a booted foot into a small crack, and hoisted himself up. This time he kept his long arms extended so his torso was five feet from the coiled reptile.

A Mojave green was the deadliest of the many inhospitable creatures of the desert. His horned, scaled head lay on the coils of his small, but thick body. The green flicked its forked tongue lazily as it tested the air for the intruder's scent.

Ned balanced on one foot. His left arm, swung out away from the cliff face. He removed his broad-brimmed hat with his free hand and sailed it atop the resting reptile. Even though he was anticipating the snake's wicked buzz, the chilling sound almost caused him to lose his grip and crash to the outcropping below.

The snake hurriedly found a crevice and, buzzing in anger, disappeared.

Ned hoisted himself up onto the ledge once more. Getting one knee up, he pulled himself, panting, to safety. He had torn his left hand badly. Only the wedged hand had saved him. Stripping the red kerchief from his neck, Ned wrapped his bleeding hand, pulling the knot tight with his teeth. His breath came in ragged gasps. He spit to get the sour taste of fear from his mouth.

He climbed higher into the domain of the chuckwalla lizards, sand lizards, plus the occasional whip-tail — and the snakes, of course, which fed on them as well as on the rats and mice of the lower slopes. Even higher up the cliff face were the nests of ravens. Higher still were those of the hawks and falcons. Almost at the very top, on a ledge not far from where Cody finally came to rest, a family of golden eagles lorded over all.

Ned surveyed his surroundings. The rounded shoulders of the dome became smooth wind-worn basalt cliffs, promising death to all who tried to scale them. Ominous and foreboding, they challenged all but the very bravest — and the most foolhardy. The dome — the Devil's Bowler — was well named.

Ned shifted the Winchester .44/.40 slung across his back to a more comfortable position. He knew he had to hurry. If he didn't reach the top of the dome before full light, his quarry would be gone again. It all wouldn't matter anyway if Ned didn't get back to water in a very few hours.

Cody was fairly sure Saragosa knew he was being tracked. But if surprise was possible, Ned wanted the first shot fired to be the last. And he wanted to be the one to fire it.

The top of the dome loomed fifty feet above him. The wind howled, pulling at him to keep him from reaching the summit. Its moaning cry was a warning. One to be taken seriously. Garnering his strength, Cody ignored his cut and bleeding hands and aching arms and shoulders, and looked around for a route to the top.

A noise pulled his attention upward. He flattened himself against the cold rock face, crouching near a shadowed hole that proved to be an opening to a broader cave. Unslinging the .44/.40, he slipped into the dark crevice. His eyes adjusted to the dim light quickly as his nose recognized the acrid smell of bat guano somewhere deeper in the cavern. Ned blinked in amazement, discovering he was not the first to explore the cave. The walls were covered with colorful drawings. Cody ran a calloused hand across the smooth face of the cold rock. It was drawn on in black and red and ocher, on a huge slab where dark brown basalt gave way to a lighter gray.

Huge animals with tusks longer than the stick men beside them emblazoned the wall. The men figures carried long spears. The drawings told of a hunt. A third drawing, deeper in the cave, showed an animal prostrate, with kneeling hunters facing a circle above a horizontal line.

Ned wondered how long it had been since hunters had visited this cave. How many years had passed since their shaman had recorded this hunt. Cody guessed thousands. Maybe even hundreds of thousands.

Primitive chanting reverberated through the passageways. The eerie sound jerked him back to reality. The sound of chanting echoed in his ears. To Ned's exhausted, sun-blinded eyes, the figures on the wall began to dance with bizarre jerking movements. The floor of the cave was littered with the bones of small animals as well as regurgitated fur and feather balls. Not only bats, but owls must have been the recent residents of this shelter as well.

Ned wished he had the time to sit, rest and ponder the meaning of the drawings. The repetitive echo of the chanting nearly lulled him to sleep. But Ned slapped his own cheeks repeatedly to remain alert. A man waited above. A man in many ways akin to these crudely painted pagan hunters. But Saragosa's prey had not been the animals depicted in these drawings. His prey had been human. Eleven that Ned had heard tell of, and two that he had buried personally. And if Ned didn't get his man, there would certainly be more. A man like Saragosa never stopped. He had to be stopped.

Ned couldn't rest, not even for a minute, so he did the next best thing. He pulled the leather bag from his shoulder and took a deep draw of the warmed water. He judged there was a little more than a pint left, less than a morning's supply.

Cody sighed deeply. He wished he was lying in the hammock hanging between the twin sycamores in the front of Mary Beth's house. In Bakersfield, June temperatures might reach ninety, or even a hundred. While here, in just a few hours, it would be a hundred and twenty on the desert floor three hundred feet below. Back home, Mary

Beth would have a tall, cold pitcher of lemonade sitting on the kitchen table just in case a thirsty man happened by — Mary Beth, who had asked him time and time again to quit his job as sheriff.

Right now, he wished he had listened.

Ned steeled his resolve. The fastest way to get home, he knew, was to get the job done. He headed for the light of the cave entrance. Something fluttered by his face and he flinched. Suddenly, there were hundreds of flying creatures blackening the opening. Ned dropped to the floor and rolled to his side. With daybreak, thousands of bats were returning to the darkness of the cave. The damp, dark air of the enclosed cavern swirled with their beating wings. When the first onslaught lessened, Ned crawled out to the ledge and away from the opening. Only then did he allow himself a shudder of revulsion.

Standing, he studied his approach to the top. He adjusted the .44/.40 on his back and started up once again, gritting his teeth at the intense pain in his hands and shoulders. Hand over cut-and-bleeding hand, Ned climbed on, wondering if the next ledge would bring him face to face with Saragosa — a far more formidable obstacle than any snake or bat or sheer mountain cliff.

The slope eased somewhat. Now Cody was able to stand and walk to the top. He shook out his arms, limbering his cramped shoulders and biceps, and cautiously moved forward between two huge boulders.

The top of the dome was flat — two acres of level brown basalt broken up by three rings of small boulders thirty feet in diameter. The boulders had been carefully placed, probably by the same hunters who had painted the cave walls all those centuries earlier, as an offering to a god or gods only they knew.

In the center of the three rings, clad in loincloth and leggings, stood Mangas Saragosa. His long, thick black hair hung down to the center of his back. The tattoos covering his body bore an eerie resemblance to the cave drawings. He had his arms extended toward the rising sun and he was chanting.

Ned wondered for a moment if the man had come here to pray. Then he shouldered the .44/.40. As far as Ned was concerned, the man had come here to die.

Quietly cocking the rifle, Ned took a bead on the center of the broad, tattooed back. But try as he might, he could not fire. Ned had never shot any man in the back and he wasn't about to start now. Instead, he whistled softly, giving Saragosa a chance to turn and face his executioner.

Suddenly a thin but brilliant orange and platinum line flared across the horizon. Ned squinted into its sudden brightness. The sun cresting the Funeral Mountains in the distance created a mystic aura about the massive Saragosa.

Saragosa dropped his arms and stood frozen for a second. Then he disappeared.

Ned sighted down the barrel of the Winchester, unwilling to believe what his eyes had just told him. He spun, wondering if the Indian had somehow gotten behind him. There was nothing. He lowered the rifle, crouched, shaded his eyes, and searched the flat with his vision. He wondered if he had not fallen victim to the desert. But his eyes had not deceived him. The man was gone.

It was said that Mangas Saragosa was a demon.

A demon of the desert.

Maybe it was true.

CHAPTER FOURTEEN

While Cody had made a dry and cold camp, King Hansen was less cautious, building a huge fire that could be seen for miles. Pete could sense Frenchy's anticipation as they set up within the sight of the dome.

Sarah nervously bit at her nails, sitting near the fire, her arms wrapped around her knees, rocking. She and Frenchy had gotten into a screaming argument earlier in the day when Frenchy informed her he'd brought no opium. Now the lack was beginning to gnaw at her. Pete recognized the symptoms. He'd gone through them once himself. After a while she lay in a fetal position, her forehead beaded in perspiration, and quietly whimpered.

"Can you cook?" Frenchy asked King, realizing that Sarah would be good for nothing, after the pig-eyed man had finished hobbling the horses.

"I can roast meat and make coffee," he

answered with embarrassment. "But I never made no beans or biscuits."

"I can cook like your grandma," Pete offered. Perhaps Frenchy would see fit to take the ropes off his wrists. They were raw and bleeding and the flies and little desert wasps had pestered the wounds all day.

"If you hadn't run my Moses off, you could have had sourdough pancakes," Pete said accusingly. "I got the starter and the makin's in his pack. But, I can still make real good biscuits, Frenchy."

Frenchy hesitated a moment. Then, finally, his stomach overcame his caution. "Untie him," he ordered, motioning to King. He turned back to the prospector. "If you try to run," he growled, "I'll shoot you down for buzzard bait."

King had cut the ropes loose. Pete splashed a little of their precious water on his wrists to clean them. Then he tore away his shirttail and used the cloth to bandage his wounds.

"You gonna' cook or fuss with yourself?" Frenchy snapped impatiently.

"I'm cooking. You want me to fetch the wood?"

"No. You're not leaving my sight."

Frenchy looked at King. "Get the wood. I'm hungry," he ordered. Then he turned to the girl lying on the cold ground. "Sarah, you go off in the brush if you want to moan like that."

Sarah stopped whimpering, but continued to rock quietly.

Pete worried about Sarah as he fixed the biscuits and fried the side pork. She looked drawn and haggard, with dark circles under her eyes. Tomorrow, Pete thought, the big Indian would take care of Frenchy and King. Now if he could get him to just leave Sarah be, Pete knew he could cure her. It was the opium — or, rather, the lack of it — that made her sick. Pete knew with rest and good food, and no more of the poison smoke, the girl could again be her beautiful self.

Pete thought his best chance would be to find Saragosa and enlist his aid. He continually looked for an opportunity to slip off into the cactus. But Frenchy was watching him far too closely. Pete feared he'd end up shot, now that the Devil's Bowler was in sight and Frenchy knew where he was going. But he didn't yet know the exact location of the mine. That was a point in Pete's favor.

When supper was finished, Frenchy had King retie Pete. But it was not so bad as before, now that the bandages were in place.

They awoke to a whistling, dust-laden wind. It dried and scorched them like the hot air from a blacksmith's bellows as they ate a handful of jerky. Sarah had fed Pete as best she could, though she herself didn't eat. King loaded Pete onto the saddle, tying his wrists to the pommel and his legs to the stirrups. Then they set out toward the dome. The horses kept turning away from their into-the-wind course, but Frenchy persistently drove them on.

Ned lowered the rifle, still staring in disbelief. The sun crept higher, blinding him even more. Ned stood and moved forward, shielding his eyes with his hand. He had to find Saragosa to kill him or capture him. He had to make this end.

As Ned neared the spot where the Indian had been standing, he found the answer to the mystery. A four foot round hole sunk into the ground, almost like a well. It slanted off to the side and Ned could see only fifteen feet or so down into the darkness. Its sides were as slick as glass. Once inside there would be no climbing out. It must have been some kind of blow hole created when the mountain first formed. Ned figured that was why he had heard the chanting so clearly while he was in the cave earlier. That was where the hole must lead.

Cody had no rope. He had no torch. He had a few sulfur heads in his pocket, but figured he'd better save them. Ned was not looking forward to this. Following Saragosa into the bowels of the Devil's Bowler would be like chasing Satan into the depths of hell.

Even if he did find the Indian, what were the odds he could find his way back out? Saragosa obviously knew the mountain and its caves intimately. While one wrong turn might lead Cody to perdition.

Ned took a deep breath. He stepped off the edge and landed on his rear, immediately shooting forward and down. Sliding faster and faster, he desperately hung onto his rifle. Ned slammed suddenly into a wall, and the rifle clattered away. He reached for it, and began sliding once again. Ned skinned his hands grasping frantically at the walls, trying to slow his descent. But it was to no avail. After a while, Cody began to slow perceptibly. He slid into something sticky, which decreased his speed even more. He came to a full stop, wrapping his body around a round rock column. Then the smell hit him. Bat guano. Which meant bats.

He sat up. What the hell have I done, he thought. I could still be running a freight station for Wells Fargo. I could be fishing in the creek behind the station. He shook his head. No, he thought, I gotta be chasing a crazy, giant Indian down a snake hole. It's pitch dark and I gotta spit on my hand to know down from up . . . and I don't have much spit left to begin with. Ned wondered if peyote helped you see in the dark.

Ned collected himself. He patted around the slimy floor and located the rifle. At least it had slid along the same path as he did. Foraging through his pocket, he found a match and struck it against the wall. It did nothing but inform him what he already knew: there was darkness above and more darkness below. The match did little good and he might need his small supply later. Besides, it would tell the Indian his exact location. The noise Ned was making was bad enough. But at least it echoed up and down the cavern making it difficult to pinpoint its exact origin.

Cody knew he would never get out of there unless he got started. He tried to move quietly and efficiently, but was constantly running into walls. His boots smacked loudly in the slime covering the floors. If the Indian was waiting — and Ned was sure he was — he could no doubt hear him coming.

Ned felt like a rabbit in a badger hole.

Suddenly there were sounds from the far end of the tunnel. Ned came to a fork. By walking in a circle and feeling all the tunnel walls, he was able to determine which path went where. He was confused as to where he had come from for a moment until he realized he'd been walking downhill. Collecting himself, he mentally retraced his movements. Then he heard the sounds again and knew the way he must go. Again he walked into a rock wall. The rifle clattered loudly against the stone. He turned, and saw a flicker of light a distance off. Hell, Ned figured. If loud noise was confusing in the confinement of the tunnels, he'd be better off being as loud as possible. Nervously, Ned began to whistle, softly at first but then louder. Damn! The man knew he was coming anyway. Ned began to sing with great gusto, even though he was not sure of the words. But it really didn't matter.

Mangas had stepped into the hole, made the slide feet first and hit the floor running. He'd left his Henry rifle with the horses. If the man who followed was crazy enough to climb the sacred mountain in the dark, the Mojave wanted his Henry by his side. He'd never known a white man to face him alone, much less chase him to the top of his most sacred place.

His face and shoulder ached with every step he took.

When he got far enough along the tunnel, he recovered a torch that he'd hidden. With flint and steel from his medicine bag, he soon had it roaring. Saragosa strode quickly into the big open cavern and fetched his rifle from its scabbard. The Mexican and the big man watched him closely, but said nothing.

Mangas walked to where Ratzlaff stood, the noose tied snugly around his neck. He held the torch close to the big man's face, surprised by the inner strength that still blazed in his eyes. It will take this one a long time to die, Mangas thought. I should have killed him earlier. Holding the torch in his left hand, he drove the butt of the Henry into Ratzlaff's mid-section. The big man would have doubled over but the noose choked him and forced him to straighten up.

"You grimy gut eatin' son-of-a-bitch!" Cuen screamed from across the chamber. But Mangas ignored him. The Mexican would get his turn. Mangas kicked the big man's feet out from under him. But as Ratzlaff went down, the four inch limb above him cracked, breaking in half as he went crashing to the floor.

Mangas shook his head in disgust. So far nothing had gone right. The man who followed had made the impossible night climb to the top of the sacred mountain, interrupting his praying. The limb had broken so the big man did not hang. The Gods seemed against him today. Mangas decided to just shoot them all and drive the mules on to the Colorado.

Mangas dropped the torch and levered in a shell. Then he heard the singing echoing through the huge room.

"Buffalo gal, won't you come out tonight, come out tonight, come out tonight. Buffalo gal won't you come out tonight and howl at the light of the moon."

The crazy white man was singing at the top of his lungs. Mangas thought it must be his war chant. He turned to face the end of the cave where the sound was coming from. Quietly he brought the rifle up to his shoulder.

Mangas hated singing. The miners who'd killed his mother and father when he was a young boy, had been singing. Singing was an evil thing. And now it reverberated though his mountain.

It made Saragosa's head hurt, bringing back terrible memories he'd tried hard to forget. The singing made the fire burn in his heart — a fire that could only be squelched with the blood of a white man or Mexican.

Mangas's finger had tightened on the trigger, just as the white eye stepped into the opening at the end of the big room. Mangas centered the rifle on his chest.

Lying on the floor of the cave, Theo Ratzlaff opened his eyes. His tongue was swollen and his eyes burned from dryness, but he could still see. The Indian stood three steps in front of him, his silhouette outlined by the still burning torch stuck in the rocks just two feet in front of him.

Theo could feel the fury surging through his body. Quietly, he maneuvered his bound ankles under him. Leaning against a boulder, he struggled to his feet. His wrists were still bound, but at least in front of him.

He lunged, dragging the broken limb behind him. He dropped his bound wrists over the Indian's head and dragged him to the floor.

Saragosa's Henry roared as the hemp scraped his face. The pain from the infected, swollen, wound made the Indian scream as he was dragged to the floor by the huge weight on his back. He landed on his bad shoulder. The pain shot through his body as his Henry was knocked from his grasp. Mangas rolled and kicked and finally freed himself. The man at the end of the cavern now had his rifle leveled on him as Mangas leapt to his feet.

On the brink of unconsciousness, Ratzlaff tried to focus on the standing Indian. Lashing out with his bound feet, he caught the Indian in the back of the knees.

Cody's rifle spewed flame from its muzzle, and its roar reverberated through the huge cavern as the Indian went down, landing on top of the burning torch, searing his back. Saragosa rolled over it and screamed.

The torch went out. In the darkness, Saragosa had the advantage. No, he decided. The gods were against him.

He could hear the sounds of men on both sides of him. Saragosa decided he would find the soothing mud of the rotten egg spring and doctor his back. Then he would deal with the men.

Stealthily, he worked his way to the cave opening, and slipped into the passage. There would be another day, when his face and shoulder were well and the searing, agonizing burns on his back were healed. A day when the gods were on his side.

Mangas paused in the tunnel, and screamed the cry of the eagle.

No one was more surprised by Cody's singing than Al Cuen. At first he'd thought he was losing his mind. But as he cocked his head and listened over Ratzlaff's coughing and spitting, he distinctly recognized Ned Cody's voice. It had to be Ned. No one else sang that badly.

Once he realized the Indian was gone, Cuen yelled hoarsely, "Cody! This way!"

"Who's there?" Cody called out.

"It's me, Ned. Alvarado! Hurry, Theo's choking."

"Where's the Indian?" Cody asked cautiously.

"He went on. Hurry!" Writhing on the ground, Theo choked and coughed from the noose pulled tightly around his neck.

Al heard Cody charge into the room.

"Ned," Al gasped, "to your right about shoulder high on the wall is a torch. No! Your left, my right. Feel along the wall."

"Got it." Ned called out in the dark.

Al saw a sulfur head flare up and soon Ned had the torch burning brightly. The sheriff hurried over to Theo, quickly cutting the rope away from his neck. The big man lay on the floor gasping for breath as Ned cut his hands and arms free. Then he hustled to Al and did the same.

Al stepped away from the stalagmite, rubbing his wrists and hands vigorously. *"Madre mia,* am I glad to see you," he rasped. Catching a good whiff of his rescuer, Al wrinkled his nose. "You stink, *amigo,"* he said. Ned grimaced. Al stumbled along the wall to where the horses stood. Nudging them out of the way, he fell to his knees, immersed his face in the pothole of water and drank deeply.

"Careful, *amigo,"* Ned cautioned. "Your stomach's dried tight to your backbone. Drink slow."

Ned helped Theo to his feet and guided him over to the water. The big deputy fell to his stomach and plunged his face right next to Cuen's.

Holding the torch close, Ned realized what bad shape his two friends were in. They were gaunt and drawn, their faces blistered and their lips cracked.

"You boys look like you been rode hard and put away wet," Ned offered grimly.

"We could have used wet, *amigo,"* Al replied. Theo's face was still buried in the water. "We have been dry for most of two days. If you'd been a day later, we would be little piles of coyote and buzzard dung."

"Hell, Al," Cody said, laughing quietly. "You knew I'd be along. You still owe me five from the last poker game."

Cuen grinned. "You could have held it out of my wages, *amigo.*"

"Dang," Ned chided. "If I'd thought of that I'd still be drinkin' that cheap whiskey in Mojave."

When Theo finally raised his face from the water, Ned studied his two friends carefully. Though both were battered, they looked as if they could handle moving on. "Let's see if we can find our way out of this hole," he said. "There won't be any going back the way I came."

"We came in face down." Al offered. "But I think I can retrace our steps."

Cody nodded. "That stallion you ride will find his way out," he said. He'd always admired Al's mount. "Just cut him loose, and we'll trail along."

Ned caught a brief golden glimmer of something and walked across the room. "I'll be damned," he exclaimed, picking up Saragosa's abandoned Henry. "The Indian lost his rifle when Theo jumped him. No wonder he left! I didn't figure him for a runner on his own ground!" He carried the rifle with him as they followed Cuen's roan, big Theo Ratzlaff leaning on the two other men's shoulders for support.

Minutes later the stallion had led them to safety. The opening to the cave was only a few feet above the desert floor. The same sun that the men had cursed for days looked damned good to them now, even despite its baking heat.

"If that stallion will ride double," Cody suggested, "let's double up. I left my horse in a draw around on the north side. We got to go back and see to Big Jim Jackson. I left him with a bullet hole in his leg, lying near a water hole a few miles back."

"What about the gut eater?" Theo asked.

"You two Indian fighters need a little rest before you go another round with Saragosa," Ned answered. "I got a feeling we could hunt him forever in this hollow mountain, and he would pick us off one at a time. This place is like a maze. And it's Saragosa's maze."

"I want a crack at him, Cody," Theo growled standing shakily on his own two feet.

"I know, you'll tack his hide to the wall."

"That's right," Theo said confidently.

"Let's go find Jackson." Cody smiled. "You two can plan a new attack."

Ned looked up at the stark, treeless mountain as they circled it in the desert. "I'll be back, Mr. Saragosa," he promised quietly. "But next time it'll be on my terms."

Mangas sat on a ledge high on the mountain. His face, shoulder, and back were smeared with the healing yellow mud. Silently he watched the two horses and three riders disappearing in the distance. Luckily for them they were riding around the west end of the dome and were already three-quarters of a mile away before Mangas saw them. He'd recovered the Sharps that he'd taken from Two's Riding, and could knock a man out of the saddle at five hundred yards with the old gun. But no further.

He would not chase them. His back burned and tortured him and his shoulder and face sent tremors of pain throughout his body. Perhaps the men riding away had given up. Maybe not. Whatever the case, Saragosa would bide his time. He had the patience of the desert.

CHAPTER FIFTEEN

Before he'd climbed the mountain, Ned had left the roan, the mule, and the pinto tied in the shade of a ravine bank near where he'd camped the night before. The sage he'd tied them to was on the flimsy side. Just in case Ned didn't come back and the animals would have been able to pull themselves free and make their own way across the desert.

Ned, Al and Theo recovered the stock and headed out. It was a twenty mile trek to where Ned had left Jackson, and they rode in thirsty, cracked-lip silence despite having drunk their fill before leaving the cavern. The horses had to suffer as Ned had just enough water to wet their mouths a few times with a damp cloth. Both Cuen and Ratzlaff were too spent to talk. And Ned was lost in his own thoughts. Theo complained of dizziness and Ned figured he had a concussion. The gash in his head festered from being unattended for so long.

There was nothing Ned hated more than leaving a job undone. It was a hard three-day ride back to Mojave, but Ned knew he had to return to re-provision. Plus Cuen and Ratzlaff needed rest and recuperation. And both Theo and Jackson needed medical attention. These men were good lawmen — with the possible exception of Big Jim — but they weren't Indian fighters. Henry Clay Hammer was, however. And if Ned called, Henry would come. But he hadn't seen Henry in almost five years. Hell, for all Cody knew, he might be dead. It was always possible with a man who walked as close to the edge as Henry Clay did.

As they crossed a wide valley, the wind rose up again and whipped at them mercilessly. They covered their faces with kerchiefs and hung their heads low. Ned picked up the fading trail of another group of shod horses. He thought it curious to find sign of a group in this particular spot. The barren valley they crossed was somewhere between nowhere and no place special. Sign of anything more than a prospector and a burro was unusual.

But the group was headed to other way, toward the Devil's Bowler. But with hardly any water and three injured men to worry about, Ned wasn't about to overtake the riders and warn them to stay away from the Indian.

The sun was near the western peaks by the time they spotted the willows and cottonwoods in the distance. By the time they rode into Jackson's camp, it was well below the peaks whose shadows covered the valley.

Both the horses and men headed straight for the water hole.

"Jackson!" Ned called out after drinking his fill. The man was nowhere in sight.

"Cody?" a muffled voice called out. "Ned Cody? Over here."

Two cottonwoods stood tall and whiskered in the mess of willows — old timers, having outlived five generations of the smaller trees. Ned rode over to them.

"Boy, am I glad to see you!" Leaves rattled and bark fell from the tree as Jackson climbed down. "Damn wolves chased me up here. I been in this tree since yesterday afternoon." Jackson dropped from the lowest branch. He dragged his leg to the water hole, and fell onto his belly, burying his face in the warm, clear liquid.

"Why didn't you shoot them?" Ned asked.

"After I shot up all my shells, I feared I might fall asleep. So I figured the tree was my best bet."

"Did you kill any?"

"Don't know. They was out in the brush."

Ned shook his head disgustedly. The man had been firing blindly into the brush wasting all his shells on shadows. When all this was over, Ned swore to himself he'd find a new deputy for Mojave.

All the wood had been burned and hadn't been replaced. "I'll collect some wood," Ned mumbled in annoyance, "and get some grub together. We'll take turns standing watch tonight."

Supper was nothing but beans and pan bread, but they all ate ravenously. Ned kept the first watch. The others joined together in a snoring serenade that drowned out the distant wolves and nearby coyotes.

Mangas sat on the edge of the precipice, his back to the scorching wind, his long hair blowing and whipping in front of his face. He watched silently as four riders approached. He'd been to the rotten egg spring three times to redress his wounds. But each time he was drawn back to the top of the mountain, where he sat watching to the west. He didn't need any more stock. Mangas had as much as he could handle now. But strangers were coming to his mountain, so he would kill them.

He decided on a spot halfway down the cliff to await the riders. He went to the blow hole, slid down, and worked his way through the caverns until he came out on a ledge facing the approaching foursome. He laid the Sharps across a rock and sighted the lead rider. As they neared, he could see a woman's long hair whipping in the wind and the old prospector's horse being led — with the rider's hands tied behind him.

The old man was being held prisoner. That was the reason he'd not left his offering of shells and candy. And they had a woman with them. It had been a long time since Mangas had a woman. He decided not to risk firing at them from the high ledge. He might hit the woman or Pete. His knife could do the work just as well. He was sure they would camp near the water. When they did, they would find the mules — yet another reason to kill them. But Saragosa did not think this group came for the stock. It was the old man's gold they wanted. That was why the old man was tied up.

It was good. Here was a chance to pay back the old man for saving his life. Once he did that he could order the old man to leave the sacred mountain. The mountain had enough holes in it already. Mangas would owe him no more. And Mangas would get a woman. It would make up for losing the Mexican.

He disappeared into the mountain as they neared. Night would be a better time for action.

Working his way to the cave opening overlooking the mules, he settled down in the darkness near the opening and kept watch.

As King unpacked the mules in the shade of a solitary cottonwood, Frenchy jerked Pete from the saddle. "I want to see the mine," he demanded.

Pete eyed him skeptically. He wondered if Frenchy would kill him the instant he knew the mine's location. "You got to untie me Frenchy. We got to walk some, then climb some."

As Frenchy cut away the ropes, Sarah went to the trickling water they had camped nearby. She drank, wet her face and the back of her neck, then lay in the shade of the cottonwood. She'd been very quiet since she'd first gotten sick from the lack of opium. Every once in a while, she'd double over in pain and break out in a cold sweat.

"Pete and I are taking a walk," Frenchy called out, shoving Pete out in front of him. "You set up camp, King."

They made their way up the escarpment

to the edge of the dome. Frenchy looked back and saw a herd of mules on the upper reaches of the creek in oasis canyon. "What the hell, Polecat," he panted, already out of breath from the short climb. "Why do you have so many mules here?"

Pete hadn't known about the mules. But he knew who had brought them.

"I . . . found them in the desert, running free," Pete said haltingly. "They . . . uh . . . they came to the water in the creek and I corralled them"

A bonus, Frenchy thought smugly. A gold mine *and* twenty head of mules. "Let's find that mine!" he ordered.

The mine was around a turn in the game trail. They crawled over the small pile of tailings at the entrance, then stepped into the narrow shaft.

Frenchy smiled broadly. "A good wide vein," he admitted. "Very good, old man. I want you to show me how to use the mill and how to extract the gold from the ore. I have never mined gold, nor silver."

Pete sighed in relief. It was a reprieve. It would take a full day to teach Frenchy how to turn the ore into amalgam. That should give the Indian time to find them — if the Indian was on the mountain.

■ ■ ■ ■

Mangas watched the men work their way up the rocks until they disappeared from sight. There was something strangely familiar about the man following the old prospector. It was a familiarity that rankled Mangas and made him uneasy. He didn't understand the feeling. He sat in the darkness and searched his memory.

By the time Pete and Frenchy worked their way back to camp, King had a small cook fire going and Sarah lay rocking in a fetal position, moaning softly. She managed to raise her head as they walked into the camp. "Is the mine there?" she asked, her voice barely more than a hoarse whisper.

"Yes." Frenchy smiled, his waxed mustache quivering. "I am rich!"

"We are rich, Frenchy. *We!"* Sarah wailed. She watched him closely through deep-set reddened eyes. King looked up from hobbling the stock.

"Of course, *Cherie. We* are rich." Frenchy's smile tightened.

The smell of water had become too much for Moses who had been keeping well out of sight. But now thirst was overcoming caution. He stepped tentatively up to the creek forty yards from Frenchy's camp. Pete glanced up apprehensively as he saw Frenchy hurry to his saddle and pull the Winchester from its scabbard.

Pete started to jump up and run, thinking it was his time to die. But then he saw Moses in the distance. Before Pete could yell a warning, Frenchy brought the rifle to his shoulder and quickly snapped off a shot. The burro brayed in pain and dropped to his fore knees.

"No!" shouted Pete. He scrambled to his feet and charged across the camp, head-butting Frenchy in the stomach before he could lever in another shell. The Frenchman fell to the ground. Pete ran over to where Moses now lay on his side. Frenchy clambered to his feet and drew a bead on the old man's back as he ran. Sarah was lost in her own world and ignored it all.

King stepped forward. "No, Frenchy. You need him."

"I don't *need* any of you," he hissed coldly.

A chill ran up King's backbone as the Frenchman centered the octagon barrel of the Winchester on his forehead. Then slowly Frenchy lowered the rifle. King sighed in relief.

Pete knelt next to the animal and laid a hand on its neck. Moses brayed weakly once again, kicked his legs spasmodically, then stilled.

Frenchy walked to the burro and old man.

Pete looked up from his dead friend and eyed his killer coldly. "You rotten low life!" Pete hissed, his eyes flashing fire. But Frenchy still held the Winchester cocked and ready.

The Frenchman turned to the huge pig-eyed man who'd followed him over to the dead animal. "Tie the old man, King," he ordered. "Then butcher the burro. Burro stew will do fine for tonight."

King shook his head. "I can roast meat, but I never roasted no donkey afore. You're cooking it yourself, Frenchy." Frenchy eyed the big man, thinking he should have shot him when he had the chance. For the first time, King was beginning to talk back and think for himself.

"As you wish, Monsieur King Hansen. I will cook the stew myself. You are all poor excuses for cooks." He gave the confused looking King a hard stare. "Butcher him and bring me the backstrap when you're finished."

Pete walked a few steps into the brush, hung his head and threw up. Sarah raised her own head for a moment, as if to say something, but instead grabbed her stomach and curled once again into a fetal position.

Having heard the sharp report of the rifle shot, Mangas worked his way around the mountain to get a view of the camp. He saw nothing amiss and could not imagine what someone might be shooting at. But he knew from long experience, the white eyes often shot at shadows.

As it began to get dark, Mangas worked his way closer to camp. He edged along a wash, then crawled through a patch of screw bean mesquite. The wind still blew so he was able to move freely without being heard. As he neared the campfire glow, he lay on his belly. He watched with his eyes half closed to keep them from catching the reflection of the fire.

The old man and the girl sat off to the side, while the other two ate. Watching the man with the thin mustache, old, bitter memories came crashing down on him like a rockslide. Mangas felt his blood pound and his jaw knot. He wanted to charge from the brush and use his knife on the man then and there. But that would be too quick. This man must die slowly. Mangas would peel the skin from his body an inch at a time. It had been years, but Mangas now knew where he had seen this man before. The gods always evened things out for those who waited.

It was the man from the *Fleur-de-lis* mine. In the narrow canyon near his family's village when he was a boy. The miners had lured his village to the feast. Then, as the white eyes sang, his people were murdered.

Mangas could not believe his good fortune.

He'd lost the single Mexican only to gain the leader of the Mexicans who had killed his family. And a woman as well. He reached up and softly squeezed the medicine bag that hung around his neck.

He hoped the man enjoyed his meal. It would be his last.

Chapter Sixteen

King Hansen cleaned up his second helping of burro stew, then wiped his bowl out with desert sand. He stood and stretched.

Sarah and Polecat Pete were asleep. They hadn't eaten, but rather supped on a cup of coffee, *sans* sugar, as Frenchy haughtily pointed out.

Leaning back against a log, lying on top of his bedroll with his empty bowl balanced on his stomach, Frenchy began to snore quietly.

King needed to relieve himself. Quietly, he tiptoed past Frenchy and out of the camp into the mesquite. The day's wind had blown the haze from the desert valley, and the stars looked like you could reach up and collect them.

King wandered twenty paces into the mesquite before unbuttoning his trousers. He gazed up at the diamond-peppered sky as he watered the dry, pebble covered desert floor.

All of a sudden he was gargling on hot blood. He tried to yell out but couldn't. Blood sprayed in a geyser in front of him, covering his hands as he reached up. With a thump he fell onto the blood-soaked pebbles. He rolled to his back and tried to rise. The last thing King Hansen saw was a yellow-mottled, misshapen man with wild hair, standing over him holding a blood-smeared knife.

The stars seemed suddenly faded and far away. Then they were gone forever.

Pete awoke with a start, realizing his hands were untied. He sat up rubbing his wrists in amazement. His eyes widened even more when he noticed Frenchy hog-tied and gagged. The Indian sat cross-legged near the fire, eating stew from a bowl. His face was badly swollen on one side, making it look as if the other side had caved in. He'd applied some sticky substance to the side of his face, his shoulder, and across his back. He looked like something that had just risen from the grave.

Pete shuddered.

Sarah slept fitfully, whimpering occasionally and fighting the thin blanket that covered her. The sun bronzed the sky but still lingered behind the mountain, preparing to transform the cold into scorching heat.

Pete climbed to his feet warily. The Indian ignored him and continued eating. The old man walked over to Frenchy, who was grunting and whining through his gag, his eyes wild with fear. Drawing back a foot, Pete kicked him solidly in the ribs. Pete looked at the Indian. The tattooed man merely nodded, grunting his approval.

Pete walked into the brush to relieve himself, then jumped back with a start. King Hansen lay on the ground, his head at an odd angle. His throat had been cut from ear to ear. His pig eyes bulged out, staring vacantly at nothing. The ground looked as if a hog had been butchered on the spot.

Pete's need was suddenly forgotten.

He walked back into camp and stared at the Indian, who ate calmly.

Remembering Moses, Pete worked his way up the escarpment to the mine. He glanced back at the Indian several times. Expecting him to object somehow. But the tattooed man ignored him. Pete realized he needed a shovel — first for Moses, then for King.

Sarah sat up, leaned to the side and retched dryly. She stumbled to her feet and saw the massive, tattooed Indian who looked as if his flesh was rotting away in yellow scabs. Sarah screamed. The Indian rose, but made no move toward her. She quieted and looked frantically around the camp, unsure of whether to run or not. Neither Pete nor King was anywhere in sight. Frenchy was on the desert floor, tightly bound. His wide eyes reflected the fear she felt.

Sarah decided to run.

Leaping up, she turned and headed into the brush, only to be stopped in her tracks, by the grisly sight of what was once King Hansen. That was when the Indian caught her. He scooped her up under one arm, pinning her arms beside her body, and carried her, kicking and screaming, back to the camp. He dropped her unceremoniously on the blanket. She watched, frozen with fear, as he walked back, sat cross-legged, and picked up the stew bowl again. Some of his yellow, slimy, rotten-egg smelling skin had come off in her hand. She tried to wipe if off on the ground, but it merely smeared along her palm. She gagged, then began to retch dryly. Her pain took over once more and she soon forgot about the Indian.

Pete ran to the edge of the escarpment with the shovel in his hand. He watched the scene in fearful anticipation. If the big Indian harmed Sarah, he would crack the man's skull with the shovel. Satisfied that she would be all right, he climbed down the rocks to where Moses lay by the trickling water, shooing away three scavenger ravens who fed on the offal, Pete began digging a grave for the faithful burro's remains.

When he finished, Pete marked the grave with a cross of mesquite. He decided to buy a proper marker in Mojave. As the rose hue of morning left the face of the mountain, Pete said a few quiet words about burro heaven. Then he returned to the spot where King lay. Only ants, wasps, and flies had seen fit to feed on the big man. Again Pete dug. This grave was not as deep nor prepared with as much care as the burro's, and Pete left it unmarked.

Pete sat and watched the Indian as he ate some beans and side meat, then joined him for a cup of coffee. When they finished, the Indian collected all the rifles and revolvers in camp and saddled a horse. He grabbed Pete by the arm and led him to the mount.

Pete looked at him in surprise.

Mangas held a Winchester loosely in one hand. He motioned Pete into the saddle. "You go."

Sarah had stopped her moaning and raised her head to watch. Her sickly stare turned to one of fear. She stumbled to her feet and screamed, running to Pete's side. "No! Please, Pete. Don't leave me."

"You go," Mangas repeated. "She stay."

"Please," Sarah cried. "I need my pipe! I'm sick! I'm so sick!" Mangas shoved her roughly to the ground. He turned to Pete.

"You go." Saragosa said. He cocked his rifle. The resounding click echoed in the morning air. Slowly Pete mounted.

"Oh, God!" Sarah tried to rise, then collapsed.

"Do not return," Mangas said, staring with cold and unblinking eyes at the wizened prospector.

Pete spurred the horse and rode on out of the camp, the sound of Sarah's screaming echoing in his ears. There was no way he could fight the huge Indian and expect to live long enough to help Sarah.

If only he had a gun.

By riding well into the night and starting out again before the next day's sun, Cody and his deputies were able to reach Mojave in three days.

Four gaunt, drawn, mounted men, two pack mules, and a saddleless pinto reined up in front of a store marked *Apothecary. Dentist, Doctor of Men and Animals, Undertaker.*

Ned slouched in the saddle for a moment before he could work up the energy to throw his leg over and dismount. Cuen followed. Together they walked beside Ratzlaff's horse. Ned offered the man a hand, but Theo shook him off. Then, with painful effort, the mammoth deputy climbed down.

Both Cuen and Ned pulled Jackson from the saddle and Al lent him a shoulder. Together all four men hobbled into the doctor's office. Townspeople had begun to gather by the time Al returned to take care of the horses. He flipped a young boy a coin. *"Muchacho,"* Cuen said. "See that these animals are cared for. Take them to the livery."

"Yes, sir." The boy smiled and began leading the first two away.

Al turned and walked into the office. The two men who'd been driving the wagons Saragosa had attacked followed him inside.

When the door closed, Ned nodded at the two newcomers.

The taller one spoke up. "Didn't see the Indian nor the mules come in with you," he observed.

Cody shook his head. "Didn't get him . . . *yet,*" he answered, too tired to elaborate.

"Hell's bells!" the man exclaimed disgustedly. "He'll be half way to St. Louie by now."

"You tend your wagon driving, friend," he said as the doctor took a soapy brush to the back of Ratzlaff's head. Theo winced.

"Dang, doctor," the deputy complained loudly. "You digging for gold?"

"Unless you want to be maggot-brained, Mr. Ratzlaff, you'll let me get this cleaned out." The doctor — a balding man in half glasses and a white apron — continued his scrubbing.

Jackson lay on a leather-covered table, his brow beaded with perspiration.

Cody stood up from the ladder-backed chair he had been resting in. "I'm going to the telegraph office," he announced. "I'll see you fellas at the boarding house across from the Silver Gunsight. We'll be headin' back to Bakersfield in the morning."

Ratzlaff raised himself up from the table and stared at Ned quizzically.

"We're just gonna catch our wind," Ned told him, anticipating his question, "and get you boys rested up."

Ned spun and headed for the door. As he reached for the handle, the door swung open. J.W.S. Perry and Delemeter, the head mule skinner from the Harmony Borax Works, stood in the entranceway.

The superintendent led the lanky skinner into the room. He nodded at Cody then surveyed the total scene. Perry reached into his waistcoat pocket and drew out a few cigars. He offered one to each man in the room. Delemeter drew a Lucifer across the leather table top — eliciting a stern frown from the doctor — and lit each man's cigar. Then he himself bit off a chaw from a lump of tobacco.

"Looks like you fellows got your fill of Saragosa," Perry said nodding. "The old Shoshone Indian and his grandson said you wasn't having much luck."

Ned didn't answer. He lowered himself once more in to the ladder-backed chair.

Perry dug into his coat pocket and removed a folded piece of paper which he handed to Cody. "I printed this up after you rode out." he said.

Ned unfolded it and read:

REWARD
FOR RETURN OF HARMONY
BORAX WORKS MULES AND
WHEEL HORSES
STOLEN BY THE HEATHEN
MANGAS SARAGOSA
$2,000 DOLLARS GOLD
$100 EACH FOR 20 HEAD OF STOCK
$1,000 DOLLARS GOLD
FOR SARAGOSA

DEAD OR ALIVE
OFFERED TO LAWMEN OR LAYMEN
CONTACT J.W.S. PERRY
HARMONY BORAS WORKS
MOJAVE, CALIFORNIA

Ned read in silence. When he finished he handed the paper back to Perry. "I'll bring him in," he promised, "reward or no reward." Ned studied the well-dressed man with a cold appraising eye. "Mr. Perry, you have no authority to offer a dead or alive reward on that man. He's not been convicted of a crime and no warrant has yet been issued by the superior court."

"Then get one issued, *Sheriff Cody*!" Perry insisted firmly, chomping down on the cigar so hard it bounded up and down between his teeth, threatening to jump its ash on the floor. "I was thinkin', maybe it's time we got the Army into this."

Ned stood up suddenly, his face red with indignation. "We're not calling the Army in to chase after one Indian, Mr. Perry!" he said, almost shouting.

"I want my mules back, and I want that Indian at the end of a rope!" The cigar danced again. "He killed two of my men!"

"We're gonna catch our breath," Ned said, keeping his anger in check. "Then we're going back out after Saragosa." Ned started for the door, then turned back. "I'm calling in a specialist in Indian affairs, Mr. Perry. He's no Army man, at least no longer, but his *is* a one man army. He and I will get the job done." With that Ned spun around and stormed out of the door. He headed immediately down the street toward the railroad station.

Delemeter and Perry followed Ned out. "I'll give you another week, Sheriff," Perry called after him. "If you don't have my mules back by then, I'm calling in the army!"

Ned stopped in his tracks. He did an about-face and stormed back. The two men stood face to face with him, their long cigars almost touching.

"Mr. Perry." Ned said quietly. "I'm sheriff of this county. It'll be me or the County Board of Supervisors who call in outside help. *If we* need it." Ned took the cigar from his own mouth and flipped it out into the street with disdain. "And *if* I need your consultation, I'm sure you'll oblige. Until then, let me do my job."

Perry's face turned beet red as Ned spun around once more and made his way across the street to the railroad station where the telegraph office was situated.

Delemeter spat a stream of tobacco into the street, then smiled at his red-faced boss. "Well, J.W., he's got grit in his craw, that's for sure. Enough to grind up a boulder."

"It's going to take more than grit to catch that tattooed devil," Perry snorted. "One week, then I'm appealing to the governor. The company didn't make over a thousand in contributions just to let some local lose me ten thousand in fine mules."

"My money's on the sheriff," Delemeter said. He smiled and spat again.

Perry turned toward his head skinner. "I got a ten dollar gold piece and the price of a steak dinner that says the Indian will continue to make a fool out of our sheriff. It'll be the Army that brings him in. I just hope he doesn't take a liking to mule meat before they get it done."

Delemeter took another gnaw at the plug of tobacco and worked it down into his cheek. "Think I'll take you up on that wager."

Perry extended his hand and Delemeter pumped it.

CHAPTER SEVENTEEN

Entering the railroad station, Ned was surprised to find a telegram waiting for him before he had a chance to ask for the paper to compose one of his own. He tore it open and read silently.

Ned Cody,
Sheriff, Kern County

Dear Ned,
Papa is having birthday celebration for me next Monday stop Could we announce you know what stop Be sure you're here. No Indian is more important than this stop

Love
Mary Beth stop

Oh, God, Ned thought. Mary Beth's birthday is only four days away. Cody shook his head. He'd never make it. And to top all, she'd decided to go ahead and announce their engagement as he'd been prodding her to do for so long. If he didn't show, there'd be hell to pay. She might never forgive him. But he had no choice. Going home right now was out of the question.

Cody composed his telegram carefully.

Henry Clay Hammer
Lazy Z Ranch
Bridgeport, California

Dear Henry stop
Need your help stop Be in Mojave in five days. stop I can wait seven, No longer stop

> Ned Cody
> Sheriff
> Kern County stop

It never entered his mind to mention the reward to the old black Indian fighter. If the message reached him and he wasn't bed ridden, about to breathe his last, Ned knew Hammer would come.

After a hot bath in a bath house out behind Ma Burdick's boarding house, Ratzlaff, Cody, and Al ate quietly at her table. They decided unanimously — to Mrs. Burdick's hearty approval — that there was nothing like a woman's cooking, as they polished off a kettle full of chicken and dumplings and a half apple pie each. After they'd finished, Cody suggested they step across the street to the Silver Gunsight for a short beer. Theo declined. He said he needed some serious sleep in a real bed. The doctor had decided to keep Jackson at his office to watch him closely for signs of blood poisoning.

A ferret of a man hurried down the bar as Ned and Cuen bellied up to it.

"What's yer pleasure, gents"?" he asked, his eyes shifting rapidly from man to man.

"Two beers," Cody answered.

They downed the first ones without taking a breath. Then Ned motioned to the man for a refill.

The man complied, then noticed Cody's badge. "You the sheriff?" he asked.

"Yes, sir." Ned extended his hand and introduced himself and Cuen.

"Heard a rumor around town that might interest you." The man leaned forward, speaking quietly so as not to be overhead by another group of men at the far end of the bar. "Word is that Frenchy LeConte, fella that owns the saloon down the street, rode out of here a few nights ago with one of his girls and one of his bar hands."

"So?" Cody took another swig of his beer.

The little man shifted his eyes down the bar. "So, they had a customer of mine with them."

"So?" Cody was beginning to get perturbed at the nervously jerking man.

"So, my customer's hands was tied to the saddle horn, and he was hatless. Polecat Pete sleeps in his hat. An' he don't ride no horse. He's walked this desert from Salt Lake City to Mexico. And he had his hands tied. Don't that seem a little queer?"

"You're right," Cody sighed. The last thing he needed was another problem. "What would this Frenchy want with this Polecat Pete?"

"Pete's got a mine somewhere out in the desert. Every month he comes into town and flashes around a poke of gold dust and nuggets." The little ferret man smiled, gnashing his teeth together nervously. "I figure Frenchy means to get that mine away from Polecat."

"Thank you," Ned told the man. "I'll look into it."

He turned to Al. "You don't suppose those tracks we crossed about three quarters of the way to the Devil's Bowler were these folks?"

Cuen shrugged. "Who's to know, *amigo*. But let me rest up a day or so, and I will hire that old Shoshone again and see if we can pick up a trail."

Cody clapped his friend on the shoulder. "No, Al. You need a rest, and that wind we had blew out any trail we could've followed." Ned grinned. "We left Bakersfield with only one deputy on duty and it's time we made sure the home front is okay. I sent for an old friend to help with the tracking and the Indian catching. This whole thing will look clearer after we get the sand out of our eyes."

They finished their beers and exited, walking over to Frenchy's Saloon to question his one-eared bartender about the owner's whereabouts. But they were able to learn nothing. When they finally got back to their cramped shared room at Ma Burdick's, they collapsed into their respective beds, falling asleep the instant their heads hit the pillows, even with Ratzlaff snoring loudly across the room.

Henry Clay Hammer sat the top rail of the breaking pen watching the angular faced foreman, Preacher Gatlin, throat hitch a hammerhead bay stallion. The stallion was fighting two other cowhands who were trying to saddle him. There'd been a day when Henry would have bet the cowhands a month's wages he could have gotten the Visalia saddle in place and cinched without anyone else's help. But those days were gone. It wasn't that Henry couldn't still do it. He just no longer felt the need to prove anything.

Preacher, his freckled rawboned hands working deftly, deftly, snugged the bay up to the center pole in the corral and hobbled and blindfolded the animal. Then he ambled away to let the young cowhand try to get the saddle into place.

Preacher winked at Henry, swept his copper-red hair out of his eyes, and mounted the fence. "Youngster's game enough. Now we'll see how game the bay is."

Once the cowhand got seated, his partner pulled the slip knot on the snubbing rope and the blindfold at the same time. The bay jumped, came down stiff-legged, then leaped again. His front feet pointed one way and his hind feet the other as he twisted furiously in the air.

Suddenly there was two feet of air open between the saddle and the cowhand's backside. By the time the boy came down, the bay was out from under him and halfway across the corral. The cowhand landed feet first and commenced running. It was a good thing too, since the bay spun, showed his teeth, and came racing up behind the hand aiming to dehide his rear end. The scrambling cowhand dove under the low rail of the fence just a half-step in front of the fighting mad stallion. Both preacher and Henry roared with laughter, rocking back and forth and slapping their thighs.

Their laughter was short-lived as the bay turned in his tracks and headed for them. They bailed off the fence, landing on the spectator side.

Hell's fire!" Preacher exclaimed, taking a swipe at the biting bay with his hat as the horse reached over the top rail to nip him. "That's one mean critter!"

Henry nodded in agreement.

Preacher Gatlin rubbed his lantern jaw thoughtfully. "I'm afraid that one may send half our crew to the sawbones afore he takes to saddle leather. If'n I had time, I'd break him just for spite. I'd show those two young colts how a real cowhand rides, but odds are, the hammerhead'll always be a biter and a head thrower." Preacher fitted his hat back in place, covering his shock of red hair.

"Turn him out," Henry said, pulling his own hat off and scratching his tightly curled, graying head. A pink scar, in contrast to his dusky black skin, ran from Henry's hairline across his left eye and down to his chin. "He'll pump some fine colts inta those mustang mares, but he'll be nothing; but trouble in a string.

"I agree." Preacher climbed up on the bottom rail. "Turn him out, boys!" he yelled across the corral to the cowhands. "He's too rank an' rawboned for my taste."

The men shrugged, then opened the corral gate.

The bay looked puzzled for a minute. Then he sprinted through the opening, his hoofs spraying clods of dirt out behind him. Kicking up his heels in triumph, he took to the fields.

A young Chinese who served as cook's helper on the Lazy Z, ran across the yard from the house. Panting heavily, he handed a telegram to the broad-shouldered black cowhand. "Cooky bring from town," the young man told him breathlessly. "Say give you."

Henry nodded his thanks, then ran his thumbnail along the flap and opened it. He read the message frowning. After a few seconds he looked up.

"Preacher," he said, handing the telegram to the foreman. "I got to have a few days off." Without waiting for a reply, Henry turned and headed for the bunkhouse to roll up.

"In a month we start bringing the stock down from the high pastures!" Preacher called to the black man's broad retreating back. "You be here!"

Henry waved over his shoulder, not bothering to turn around as he shoved the bunkhouse door open and entered.

Preacher harrumphed loudly. He knew it would do no good to argue, so he didn't bother. He also knew that if Henry didn't get back for a year, he'd still have a job waiting for him at the Lazy Z.

Two days of hard riding would take Henry Hammer as far as Bishop. From there he could take the train. The Carson and Colorado had constructed a line as far south down Long Valley as the Cerro Gordo diggings below Lone Pine. Then it would be another two days hard ride to Mojave.

CHAPTER EIGHTEEN

After Pete rode out of camp, Mangas sat cross-legged in front of a small fire and watched the fearful Frenchman with joyful anticipation. Sarah lay quietly. Her pain had receded for the moment and her eyes followed the huge Indian's every move.

Finally, after more than an hour, Mangas untied Frenchy's ankles and jerked him to his feet. He pushed him ahead, indicating Sarah to follow. When she made no move to rise, Mangas walked over and jerked her to her feet. But as soon as he released her, she collapsed. Saragosa bent low and cuffed her hard across the face. To his surprise, she simply grabbed her stomach where she lay and began rocking back and forth slowly. Again he pulled her to her feet. But this time Saragosa threw her over his shoulder, carrying her effortlessly. Sarah was too weak to fight him or even cry out. The Indian could have thrown her off a cliff and she wouldn't have flinched.

Frenchy slipped and fell twice, bloodying his head as they climbed the escarpment to a cavern opening. When they finally entered into the darkness, Mangas prodded the Frenchman forward with the barrel of his rifle.

Sarah mumbled the Lord's prayer, what she knew of it, as they moved deeper into the bowels of the Devil's Bowler.

As soon as he rode back into Mojave, Pete reined the well worn mare up in front of the rickety board and batt building that served as the assayer's office. Within the hour he'd filed his claim on the Devil's Bounty mine. He'd wanted to file the name he knew the mine was called by the residents of the little town: "Polecat Pete's Poontang Mine," but the assayer wouldn't accept it. He told Pete that "Polecat Pete's Mine" was fine, but Pete felt that left a lot to be desired.

By noon time, every miner in the district knew about Pete's filing, and most of them were packing — if they had the money and equipment, or negotiating for grubstakes if they didn't.

From the assayer's, Pete went straight to the mercantile. He bought himself a new razor and strap, a mug of shaving soap, a comb and mirror, and several sets of brand new clothes. He left a long list for the store owner to put together, the he headed for Cautious Callie's. This time it wasn't for the girls, but for the leather-lined bathtub they had on the premises. Callie had one of the only three bathtubs in the entire town of Mojave. The girls were actually disappointed when Pete cleaned up, shaved, then left without his usual regimen of taking each of them to bed.

"Under all that stink, hair and desert, he ain't a bad lookin' man," Callie mumbled as Pete walked out her front door. It was the first time in over three years that she'd gotten less than ten dollars out of the prospector. The cost of a bath was a quarter.

From Callie's — bathed and dressed in a city suit — Pete made his way to the barber. A haircut and shave cost him another twenty-five cents. Then Pete headed for the Silver Gunsight Saloon. No one recognized him when he climbed up on a chair.

"I'm hiring men," Pete announced to the crowd. "If you're good with a pick and shovel and with a gun, it's two dollars a day and found." Fifteen men immediately gave Pete their names. He bought them each a beer and told them to meet him at dawn at the livery, all ready to move out.

He walked over to the ferret-faced bar-tender.

"Good to see you, Polecat." The man set a beer down in front of him. "That's on the house. What got you to scrape the desert off? You getting' married or just goin' to church?'

"Maybe both. But first, I need to hire a couple of shootists, a cook, and some mule-teers."

"You may be in luck." The bartender glanced down the bar. "Shank Scroggins and his brother, Buffalo, were in here last night. They claim they head-shoot the game they bring in. They're camped out at Joshua Wells."

"They handy with a Winchester?"

"The best. They're meat hunters. They been hunting the east slope of the Sierras, providin' meat to the miners."

Pete downed the beer, thanked the man, and headed out.

By dawn, the street in front of the Silver Gunsight was crowded with men. Pete had the Devil's Bounty Mining Company fully staffed. Fifteen men who claimed mining experience, two skinners and hostlers and a Chinese cook were going along for the ride. In addition were a pair of bear-sized hunters with two rifles each in scabbards behind their saddles and two revolvers hanging on each of their pommels. Each man carried a bone-handled bowie knife on one hip and a skinning knife on the other. They were the highest paid members of Pete's entourage.

A pair of two-team equipment wagons were loaded above the side boards with lumber and supplies. A flat bed six-team wagon sat lined with plank benches to carry the men and their personal gear. Plus a total of eight mules were being packed. A three hundred gallon water wagon trailed the flat bed. Pete had purchased every firearm in town and most of the food and equipment. By ten the caravan was ready and set out on its Journey.

Peter William Stone — no longer even remotely resembling the miner who was known as Polecat Pete — led the company of men on a new purchased palomino gelding. A fine rough-out Visalia saddle and Spanish bridle gleamed with silver conchos beneath him. A crimped, fawn-colored wide-brimmed Palo Alto had covered the bald spot on his head and his now well-trimmed hair. His newly barbered Van Dyke beard was streaked with gray — once a dirty gray, it had now miraculously become a distinguished gray. He wore knee-high polished boots, beige riding pants circled by a black leather belt into which was stuffed a billowy white linen shirt. Tied on behind the saddle was a soft black leather coat.

Behind Pete rode the buckskin clad Scroggins boys. Now that Pete was scrubbed and clean, he could smell the rancid stink of the meat hunters, and wondered if he himself had smelled that rank. When Pete had ridden to Joshua Wells to hire them, he'd asked them if they'd ever killed anyone.

"Lost count with the war and all," the older of the two, Shank, had answered, eyeing Pete suspiciously. The law had long figured they killed bear, deer, and antelope for their meat, and men who crossed their trail for their money. But it wasn't a question you asked men like the Scroggins brothers right out.

Behind the Scroggins trailed two strings of mules, followed by the wagons. Both in front and behind the Devil's Bounty Mining Company rode and walked over a hundred miners setting out to see if the Devil's Bowler held their own glory holes.

The cadre of miners saw a new man astride the palomino — one who had once been an old, one burro, one blanket prospector. This was Peter William Stone. Suddenly men who had called him Polecat now called him Mr. Stone — an educated mining engineer who'd lapsed for a while and let the desert sands creep over him.

Stone had decided he wanted a woman. It had been a long time since he'd made that particular decision and the first and only other time he'd dome so hadn't worked out well. This time, he decided, things would be different.

The only things standing between him and Sarah McKinnes, was the devil's opium — and Peter Stone had whipped that villain before — and one huge tattooed Indian.

Cody's personal business in Tehachapi was not really personal.

He'd decided that to catch an animal, you needed an animal — or animals. He'd heard of the English sending beagle hounds into rabbit warrens to flush out their prey, and basset hounds into badger holes. Why not send hounds in after a man hiding in a maze of caverns? He'd heard of a bear hunter who had hounds he claimed could track anything, including humans.

The hunter was reputed to be in Tehachapi. But when Cody started snooping around town he found that the man lived far up on Bear Mountain. Ned rented a horse from a friendly rancher and set out to find the dog owner. It would cost him an extra day — a day he'd hoped he might use to go to Bakersfield and explain to Mary Beth why he wouldn't be at her birthday party, and, consequently, why they needed to postpone the engagement announcement.

Sarah kept falling in and out of consciousness. Only occasionally did she realize what was happening around her. But then she was so ill that she didn't really care whether she, or anyone else, lived or died.

Sarah looked over at Frenchy. She had never really liked the man. But dying was one thing, and what Saragosa was doing to Frenchy was another. She hadn't disliked the saloon owner enough to want to watch him tortured. Frenchy hung from a willow pole, his wrists tightly tied and tears running from reddened eyes. His mouth gagged. She looked at him and was briefly touched with sympathy. But then the pain returned and Sarah was aware of no one else's torture save her own.

The sound of Frenchy's muffled whimpering joined with Sarah's keening and echoed throughout the cavern.

The huge tattooed Indian had three torches and a cooking fire lit and the cavern flickered with shadows.

Mangas walked to Frenchy. The Frenchman's eyes opened wide. His whimpering stopped for a moment and he stared in terror. The Indian pulled a knife from his belt. He held the blade between his thumb and forefinger, so just the knife's tip was exposed. In a flash he ran the knife tip down Frenchy's chest, cutting the shirt open and exposing white flesh. A thin red line formed along the knife's path.

Frenchy gargled in gagged fear.

Saragosa ripped the shirt away. As quickly as before, he slashed the tip of the knife vertically across Frenchy's chest. A second line of blood ran parallel to the first.

The Indian sliced a line across the top of the two parallel lines. Then reaching over, he hooked the skin between his thumb and forefinger, and peeled it downward. Frenchy's eyes bulged as he let out a muted scream.

Sarah moaned in harmony, beads of sweat forming on her forehead.

Mangas quickly cut two more lines on the other side of Frenchy's chest, and peeled a foot long, belt-wide swatch of skin away. Both wounds welled up with blood, and Frenchy passed out.

Sargosa's eyes filled with hatred. He put his face only a foot from Frenchy's and screamed the cry of the eagle. Then he turned to where Sarah lay, rocking quietly. Mangas walked over to her and straddled her. He bent down and, with well-muscled arms, pulled her up to him. Sarah screamed, clawing at his face weakly.

Saragosa slapped her viciously, knocking her to the floor. She was barely conscious when he tied her wrists, hooked them over a low stalagmite and pulled her pants down to her ankles.

He hauled her up on her knees, then mounted her like an animal. After pleasing himself, he left her moaning softly on the smooth cavern floor.

CHAPTER NINETEEN

Arriving in Mojave covered with trail dust, tired and thirsty, Henry Clay Hammer tied up the buckskin gelding in front of Frenchy's Saloon. He held a small bore .25/.35 Winchester casually at his side. Slinging his saddlebags over his shoulder, he crossed the boardwalk and entered the swinging doors. Without ceremony, he walked over to the bar, propped up the rifle, and dropped his saddlebags to the floor.

A puffy-faced, one eared bartender slapped a towel down in front of Henry and eyed the black cowhand evilly.

"Gimme three fingers of anything that'll cut the five days of dust that's sittin' in my throat," Henry said quietly.

The room, which had been buzzing with noise when Henry first entered, was dead quiet now. Henry turned to survey the ten or so men occupying the tables and the four joining him at the bar. He was the only man of color in the place.

"You'd fit right in over at Sergio's Cantina," the bartender snarled. "It's two blocks behind, next to the stockyard."

The heat rose up in Henry's face. Keeping his anger in check, the old Indian fighter spoke softly. "I'd be pleased to try it out, young fella, soon as I have one dust-cutter here."

"Folks here," the fat bartender said, his eye twitching fiercely, "is mostly of a secessionist persuasion. Frenchy don't allow me to pour for coloreds. So you just move on now."

Henry shrugged his shoulders. He bent down and grabbed the Winchester by the stock, and laid it across the bar. "My friend and I have been riding for quite a spell," Henry said patting the shiny receiver of the rifle. "He says I'm gonna have one drink afore we find a more friendly bar."

"Jackson!" the bartender called out. Suddenly three men stepped back from the bar. A fourth stood at its end. He limped down the bar to where Henry waited.

Big Jim Jackson tapped the star on his chest. "I'm the law here," he announced. "And if Frenchy don't want to serve coloreds in his place, he don't have to. Now you git!"

Henry eyed the taller, younger, broader man. "If you're the law, where's Ned Cody?"

"Our peckerwood sheriff has gone back to Bakersfield where he belongs. Now you get on outta here! I ain't gonna tell you again!"

Henry had resigned himself to leaving without the drink. But there was something about this deputy that particularly galled him. And he didn't much like the one-eared bartender either. He turned his back on the big deputy and looked the bartender squarely in the eye. "Pour me that drink," Henry said, "an' I'll secede right on out of here and down the street."

The bartender reached quickly under the bar. At the same instant, Henry swung the Winchester, catching the bartender across the side of the head with the stock, splitting his one good ear open. The shotgun the bartender had been reaching for clattered to the floor behind the bar. The shock fired both barrels, blowing a hole right through the bar and hitting Frenchy's Arc de Triomphe picture on the far side of the room.

Jackson pawed for the Colt .44 at his waist. Henry drove the butt of his Winchester into the soft part of Jackson's belly. The big man fell forward. As he fell, Henry pulled the .44 from Jackson's holster. The deputy rolled to his side, holding his stomach with both meaty hands, gasping for breath.

The bartender stood against the back bar, holding the side of his face. Blood gushed between his fingers. "You black bastard!" he screamed. "That was my good ear!"

"And now I'm gonna shoot it off, if'n you don't pour me that drink." Henry ordered quietly. He never raised his voice, and he didn't now. "You might look a little better if'n you had a matched set of ear holes. Now pour it."

As Jackson climbed to his feet, gasping wheezing, the one-eared bartender filled a glass with three fingers of whiskey for Henry. The grizzled Black swallowed it down quickly. Then he put a coin on the bar, draped the saddlebags over his shoulder, shouldered his rifle and backed out the door.

Two young boys were playing in the street near where Henry'd tied his horse. Henry swung the saddlebags in place, sank the Winchester in its scabbard, and shoved a foot in the stirrup.

Jackson came crashing through the swinging doors onto the boardwalk. "You son-of-a-bitch!" he screamed. "Now reach for that rifle!" He held the bartender's scattergun leveled on Henry.

Henry dropped the foot from his stirrup and stepped back onto the street, staring into the sawed-off twin barrels. "You fire that thing and you're likely to hit these youngins," he pointed out softly.

"That's your choice friend," Jackson sneered. "Now you turn around and put both hands behind your neck."

Henry eyed the big deputy with disgust. He sighed, and did as he was told. Jackson stormed over to Hammer, his boots crunched in the sand. Then he slammed the butt of the scattergun into Henry's kidneys. The old Indian fighter was unconscious by the time he hit the dirt street.

CHAPTER TWENTY

Henry awoke on the floor of what served as the jail in Mojave. He watched as a white-footed mouse crossed the cell in front of him. It sniffed and nibbled at the chunk of bread that was half in and half out of a pan of water. Then it scampered away into a crack in the adobe wall.

Sitting up, Henry winced at the pain in his side. He got to his feet shakily. Touching his face, he realized he must have taken a bad beating. He had knots on his head, a split under his eye, and a loose tooth. This is one bad son-of-a-bitch, he thought sarcastically, beating the hell out of a man while he's unconscious.

Henry focused his eyes on the room. Crisscrossed flat iron bars separated two cells, each with an outside door. And that was it. Hell, he thought, even Independence has a better jail than this. The only light entered from narrow slots in the doors.

Henry looked out. He could see the sun setting. He placed the pan of water where he could find it in the dark. The slop bucket he moved under the bunk, which consisted of rawhide lashings across a simple frame.

He decided to relieve himself while he could still see. His water was black with blood.

Nice of Cody to invite me down, Henry thought bitterly. Then lay on his back on the bunk and stared at the ceiling.

Just after the sun arose, Peter William Stone surveyed the breaking of camp. He was surprised how naturally he had taken to directing a company of men. They formed up and moved out on his orders. By now they were close to the mountain, arriving there by noon. He waved the Scroggins boys up beside him as he took the lead position.

"You fellas ever heard of an Indian named Mangas Saragosa?"

Shank shrugged. "Can't say as we have," he answered. The bigger and older of the bear-sized pair, he did all of the talking. Peter had never heard his brother do anything more than grunt.

"Well, he's wanted by the law," Pete went on. "It's my understanding there's a handsome reward for him and for some mules

266

he stole from the Harmony Borax Works. If you fellas get a chance to take him, the reward's all yours. But he's got a woman with him. A woman I don't want to see hurt. Do you understand?"

"How big is this reward?" Buffalo asked, leaning forward in the saddle. Pete looked up, startled. He had honestly believed the man to be dumb.

"It doesn't matter if you hurt the woman," Pete said his eyes as cold and hard as those of the man to whom he spoke. "But it'll be plenty big if you don't hurt her. Because I'll throw in five hundred dollars myself."

Shank guffawed happily. "Hell man," he exclaimed, "I'd bring you a half dozen grizzly bears for that kinda money!"

"If you knew this Indian," the prospector warned, "you'd think the grizzlies were easy! So don't be getting so cocky."

The meat hunter laughed, displaying his rotting yellow teeth. "I was huntin' Injuns long before I went to huntin' bears, Mr. Stone," he said, grinning. "There never was an Injun what could take a Scroggins — rasslin', knife fightin', or foot racing!"

His brother grunted his approval. Pete frowned, but said nothing.

CHAPTER TWENTY-ONE

Mangas paced the high edge of the cliff. He'd never seen so many white men in one place as were now gathered at the foot of his sacred mountain. And they were not just infesting the north face, which is where Saragosa was looking. He'd been all over the top of the mountain. Everywhere he looked, men were swarming below. Tents had been erected in the mesquite flats and alluvial wash beds on all sides of the dome-shaped mountain.

He stood on the edge of the precipice and watched the men below climbing up the escarpment. They stopped to investigate the fallen rock, poking and chipping at the mountain with small handpicks.

Saragosa cursed to himself. He should have killed the old man years ago.

The first men he'd seen, he'd had lined up in the sights of his Winchester. But before he could fire, more intruders appeared. Finally he decided he flat out didn't have enough shells to kill them all.

Maybe if I kill a few of them in the night, he thought, the rest of them will go away. Maybe he could drive the mules out in the darkness, and just leave. But that would mean leaving the sacred mountain, and probably never being able to come back. No, he would kill a few first and see what happened. Besides, his prisoner would take another two days to die, provided Mangas was careful with him.

And he would be careful. It was two days Mangas planned to enjoy.

For the second time in two weeks, Ned swung down from a train car onto the board platform of the Mojave station.

A thin, wiry man followed. The top of the man's floppy hat came up no higher than Cody's shoulder, but the quick assuredness of his movements labeled him as all business. They walked to the livery together. The attendant led Dancer to Ned, then returned to the car with the wiry little man close behind. Again the attendant descended the ramp, this time leading a small, scarred, rawboned bay. Behind him, the small man appeared leading three strange looking dogs. The canines came up to the man's hip and must have weighed as much as he did. One dog began snapping at the others and the man separated them. He descended the ramp leading two on one side and the snapper on the other.

"I swear, Rosco," Ned said, shaking his head in amazement at his newly appointed deputy, Rosco Rawlins, the Tehachapi bear hunter, "those are the strangest lookin' dogs I've ever seen. Are you sure they'll track a man?"

"Their mama was the finest red coon hound in Tennessee," Rosco said proudly. "And their papa was a German Rottweiler who would fight a she bear, an' win! They'll track a snow flake in a blizzard if they get a scent. They'll find your Indian or you owe me nothin'."

Cody nodded. "That's fair enough." The sheriff pointed down the street. "If you want to eat, I'd suggest Ma Burdick's. I'm gonna check an' see if my man has got to town. We'll be leaving right after lunch."

"I don't give a hoot about eatin'," Rawlins said, "but I got to feed these dogs or they'll be eyein' you and me." The little man pointed toward a tamarack grove near the train station. "You can find me snoozin' in the shade a' that tree when you're ready to make tracks." With that, he led his scarred mustang to a trough and let him drink while attempting to keep his skittish, fighting dogs apart.

Ned saddled up, mounted, and headed down the street toward the saloon. He stuck his head in the door and saw the ferret-faced bartender sweeping up nearby. Asking if the bartender had seen a grizzled, scarred black man about, Ned received a shrug of the shoulders in reply. Ned headed down the block to Frenchy's.

The round-faced bartender, a white cloth tied around his head, looked up from the bar in front of Ned. "What can I get you?" he asked.

"Beer and an egg," Cody said, staring at the man's bandage. "And a little information. I'm expectin' a man. I wondered if you'd seen him. A little shorter than me, broader, scar from here to here." Ned ran a finger from his forehead to his chin as the bandaged bartender poured him a beer.

Setting an egg next to Ned's beer, the bartender snarled, "You left out blacker than Tom Crow."

Ned smiled. "He's black, that's a fact."

"He rapped me up side my head with his Winchester 'cause I wouldn't pour him a drink."

Ned laughed. "A few days in the saddle

always did make Henry a might grumpy. You know where I can find him?"

"Jail," the bartender grunted. "He's lucky Jackson didn't blow his guts all over the street. If I'd a' got my eyes to stop rollin' around in my head afore he left, I'd a' come over this bar and beat his black ass till he was nothin' but a grease spot on the floor."

"Well, one of you's lucky," Ned said, downing beer. He took the egg, dropped a quarter on the bar, and headed for the street.

Cody couldn't believe that Jackson had jailed Henry Clay Hammer. Not that the deputy probably didn't have a good reason. Henry could get a little out of temper at times. Ned was just surprised that Jackson had been *able* to jail him.

The jail was a separate, free standing adobe shack squatting behind a clapboard building housing both the town barber and the Mojave sheriff's office. Ned clattered up the boardwalk and flung open Jackson's door. The big man was not at his desk. Ned stuck his head into the barber shop where a walrus mustached man stood stropping a razor, above an unidentifiable, steaming-towel-covered customer. "You fellas seen Jackson?" he asked.

Receiving a silent negative shake of the

head, Ned strode out and around the building to the adobe shack. He peered into the slotted openings in one door, then realized it was unlocked. It creaked as he shoved it open and stepped inside. Through the crisscrossed bars separating the cells, he saw Henry Clay Hammer rise to a sitting position on his cot.

Ned sat in one cell, and surveyed his old friend through the bars. "Is there an old buffalo soldier under those knots?"

"You got a key to that door, Cody?" As usual, Henry spoke quietly. The Black man's anger manifested itself with a bulging good eye. And right now Hammer's good eye was nearly popping out of its socket.

"You may find this a little strange, Henry, but I don't. And I can't seem to locate my deputy at the moment."

Henry's eye bulged even more. "Then find the blacksmith," he said quietly but firmly. "Cause I'm not real partial to spending another minute in this hole you call a jail."

Ned stood and took the two steps toward the door. The he stopped and thoughtfully turned back to his friend. "Henry, you gotta promise me one thing before I run down a key or the smithy."

Hammer sighed. "I won't shoot your ugly, gimpy deputy, Cody. At least not till our work's done, whatever it is."

Ned smiled at his old friend. "Thanks, Henry. I knew I could depend on you." He turned and left the jail.

The smithy Ned returned with had the padlock off in two minutes.

Ned pumped Henry's gnarled hand happily. Then the sheriff went into Jackson's office and recovered Henry's .25/.35 and his saddlebags. Together they went on to Ma Burdick's. They corralled Rosco Rawlins on the way and the three of them went on inside. The aroma of baking bread made Ned's mouth water. Ma stuck her head out of the kitchen as they sat at one of the two dining tables located in what had been the living room of the old house.

"Howdy, Sheriff," she said cheerfully. "You fellas want a bowl of stew?"

"Yes, ma'am," Ned said, removing his hat and smiling.

"What do you think about the big strike, Sheriff?" Ma Burdick asked a few minutes later as she served up three heaping, steaming portions of beef stew.

Cody looked up. "Strike?" he said.

"Polecat Pete filed a claim finally. Half the town is riding out for the Devil's Bowler."

Ned turned to Henry and Rosco. "Eat up quick boys," he said. "We're riding out of here as soon as your bowl's clean."

While Henry and Rosco worked over their food at Ma Burdick's, Ned was busy arranging for a pack mule. He appealed to Delemeter, as every other animal in town that could be rented or bought was long gone. He didn't need a guide. Cody knew where he was going. And this time he was taking the finest buffalo-soldiering, Indian-fighting tracker who ever rode with the Eleventh Cavalry.

Before they headed out, Cody hurried over to the telegraph office and sent a message.

Sheriff's office
Bakersfield, Calif
Ratzlaff Cuen stop
Decided to return to Mojave stop
Take care of things there stop
Ned Cody Sheriff
Kern County Calif stop

Three mounted men, a loaded pack mule, and three strange looking dogs set out into the blistering desert just after the sun reached its high point.

The trail was covered with wagon and stock tracks from the men on their way to the Devil's Bounty bonanza. Men were still coming. Ned just hoped he would catch up with them before they reached the pot-shaped, cave-riddled mountain.

Peter William Stone wanted to take all his men and rush into the caves of the Devil's Bowler to find Sarah. But he knew better than to try such foolishness. He'd spent the first morning organizing camp and laying out the location of his smelter and mine office. When he'd first discovered the Poontang, he'd set up corner markers for four claims, even though he'd not filed them for three years. Now he placed a man with a Winchester atop each of four piles of rock at the corner of the eighty acres encompassing those claims. They spent a full morning fending off prospectors who wanted to cross the boundaries.

After the noon meal, Pete stood up and rapped on the makeshift table. "I haven't told you men this," he said once the men had quieted. "But there's an Indian who lives on, or I should say *in,* the Devil's Bowler. There's a grave over near the creek of a man some of you may know — King Hansen." Pete let the men's shocked buzzing run its course before continuing. "The Indian cut King's throat, just because he was here. Always keep your firearms close by, and keep an eye peeled. He's got a woman with him, a white woman. Some of you men may know Sarah McKinnes, from Frenchy's Saloon." The crowd commented loudly to one another. Pete waited, then went on. "This Indian may have Frenchy too, but I figure he's gone the way of King Hansen by now. There's five hundred dollars for the man, or men, who bring that woman to me in one piece." Again the men muttered among themselves. It was as much money as most of the men would make in a year working Peter Stone's mine. The man who was called Polecat Pete raised his hands for silence. "But first you men do your work," he said. After all, he had professional hunters looking for the Indian and Sarah. "I don't want any man going into the caves after that Indian. Only if you see him outside, on the mountain, do you stop work."

Mangas moved around the perimeter of the mountain top. Men had erected tents and were picking at the ground in every direction he looked. By afternoon, one man had climbed halfway up the cliff side.

Mangas stood at the top of the cliff and waited. Just as the man pulled his chest up on the cliff's top edge, Mangas stepped forward. The man looked up in surprise. Before the miner got out whatever it was he was going to say, Mangas kicked him in the throat, sending him bouncing back down the cliff face a hundred feet to the rock ledge below.

It was Mangas's mountain, and his amazement and surprise at the number of men who now surrounded it was turning rapidly to anger. The fire in his heart was beginning to roar.

The torches had burned down to dim red glows in the darkness since the Indian had left earlier. Sarah lay with her hands tied around a stalactite. Through her pain and nausea, Sarah wondered when Frenchy would die. The Indian had removed Frenchy's gag to enjoy his screams. They made Sarah sick to her stomach, compounding the terrible sickness she felt due to the lack of opium. She wondered if the Indian would start on her as soon as Frenchy was dead.

He'd allowed her to clean up at the pools of water, during one of her better spells. But feeling a little better was a mixed blessing for he now had tied her wrists and ankles when he left.

She wished, for his own sake, that Frenchy would die. But the Indian was obviously intent of keeping him alive. He was feeding Frenchy a little flour and water and giving him drinks of water each time before beginning to torture him again.

Where the hell was Polecat? Sarah wondered. Surely the old man had gone back to Mojave to get the deputy sheriff to form a posse and come back for them. And maybe, just maybe, he would bring her some opium. But then again, they had forced Polecat to show her and Frenchy and King his mine. She had been the cause of all his recent misery. Maybe he wouldn't return with anyone. But she had one thing going for her that Frenchy did not. The Indian had been using her. After the first time, it hadn't been so bad. Maybe if she worked hard at keeping his interest, she wouldn't end up like Frenchy. She shivered again at the thought of Frenchy's raw, weeping body. Almost as if in response, Frenchy moaned.

God, she wanted to see the sunlight.

Then the cramps and nausea hit her once again. It felt to her like a thousand cave rats gnawing at her belly. And, for the time being, Frenchy and the Indian were forgotten.

Cody pushed hard, which drew no complaint from Henry. It was well after dark when they came upon a camp of four men, and Rosco insisted they stop. His dogs' foot pads were getting sore and they were beginning to limp.

"Hello the camp," Ned called out as they approached the fire.

The men answered and invited them in. Ned was not surprised to find that their destination was the Devil's Bounty bonanza. A big strike, they said.

Later that evening, as Cody climbed into his bedroll, he wondered what the hell he would find when he got back to the mountain. If hundreds of miners were invading his mountain, surely the Indian would be long gone with the mules.

He turned over and faced Henry, who lay with his head propped against his saddle, rolling a cigarette. "I don't like the sound of this miner thing," Cody told him. "Our man may have hightailed it out of his mountains, if a bunch of prospectors are pecking away at it."

"If he has," Henry said, yawning, "he'll leave track. If he don't, you're liable to have a lot of dead miners on your hands. Either way, we'll find him if you want him."

"Want him?" Ned exclaimed. "I wish he'd never been born! But I *gotta* bring him in."

The dogs began to answer a coyote's howl, straining at their tethers. Ned was about to tell Rosco to shut them up when the wiry little man sat up from his bedroll. "Ain't that a sweet sound?" he said wistfully. "It's the sound of the hunt. I'd take it over the sound of a church choir anytime."

Ned grunted for an answer. He covered his head with his coat and tried to sleep.

Chapter Twenty-Two

Sarah realized she was beginning to go a little loco. She'd been in the dark cave for so long, she couldn't tell day from night. Most of the time her only company had been the raw, seeping, moaning mess that once was Frenchy LeConte. Now when he moaned and attempted to talk through bleeding lips, she *giggled* madly in response.

Saragosa came and went often, bringing pitch-covered mesquite branches for torches and dry twigs for fires. He ate things Sarah had never seen eaten before. He ground mesquite beans to make unleavened bread, roasted the fine white meat of the sidewinder over low coals, and roasted bird eggs without breaking the shells. All of it nauseated her. But the lizards were even worse. She retched at the sight of him crunching their small bones.

He left her untied. Even if she had been able to rise, she had no idea what way was out. In a rare moment of control, she had managed to get to her feet to give the Frenchman water and food. But she made no attempt to untie him. Not that it would have done any good. He was in no condition to walk, much less run away.

Men were swarming all over Saragosa's mountain.

They camped outside oasis canyon, where the creek disappeared into the desert sand. On the second day after they'd begun arriving, Mangas had watched over the mules from just inside a tunnel high above.

Two of the miners had made their way up the creek, past Saragosa's fence. He had let them get near to where the mules were grazing, then shot them both. No one had come up the canyon since, other than the man he had allowed up to drag their bodies back out.

Saragosa's shoulder had begun to mend. The swelling in his face had gone down considerably, and the blisters on his back had been transformed into scabs. The rotten egg mud was once again performing its wonders.

The Frenchman had lived longer than Mangas intended. The next day, Saragosa decided, he would take his victim to the top of the mountain and offer him to the gods. The sacrifice would end his suffering and Mangas could, at long last, drive the mules to Colorado. He'd decided to take the woman with him. He could stay here for many moons and never kill all the white men who now swarmed over his mountain like insects.

He would only kill the ones who got in his way.

But after he sold the mules, he would be back.

When the first miner had fallen to his death from the high cliffs, it had been presumed an accident. But when one of Peter's men ran into camp and reported the shooting death of two of the Devil's Bounty company miners, Peter decided to call a meeting.

The Scroggins boys had been hunting Mangas Saragosa for two days, scouting the mountain, locating caves, and looking for sign. Though they packed the latest in miner's lamps, as of yet they had not attempted to search the caves. The Scroggins boys, as Shank pointed out to Peter Stone, had not lived as long as they had hunting the California grizzlies — the most ferocious animals on the continent — by being careless. And they assured Peter that it was only a matter of time before they found a fresh trail and had the Indian's hide in their possession.

But men had died. So Pete had called a meeting.

The miners congregated at the framework of the new one-room office of the Devil's Bounty. The office stood at the edge of the escarpment, fifty feet from where the steepest of the Devil's Bowler cliffs rose over a hundred feet straight up.

Standing on a plank laid across two sawhorses, Peter William Stone called over one hundred men to attention. Some of the group had taken seats on the rocks of the escarpment. Some stood.

"Men," Pete began, "you know why I've called you together. We have a mutual problem . . . and his name is Mangas Saragosa.

"I've got no proof that these men were killed by the Indian Saragosa, but I do know he killed King Hansen right over there by the creek. I also know that those mules up in the canyon are the ones stolen from the Harmony Borax Works . . . and that was said to be the work of Saragosa."

As the crowd hummed with excitement, Peter Stone continued. He suggested an organized search through the labyrinth of caves. An argument ensued, continuing until a piercing scream from the top of the mountain hushed them all.

One hundred men shaded their eyes and looked up. High on the cliff top, with the sun at his back, stood the massive Indian. He lifted Frenchy LeConte high over his head. He hesitated a moment, then tossed the bloody parcel far out in front of him. Only the flailing arms and legs identified the falling mass as a human being.

The mess of bloody red flesh seem to soar, then plummeted one hundred and seventy five feet, careening off the cliff side before splattering to a halt in the boulders ten feet from where Shank Scroggins stood. The Scroggins boys scrambled for their rifles, but Saragosa had vanished as quickly as he had appeared.

The wind rose and wailed mournfully as the crowd stared in frozen silence.

Ned Cody, Rosco Rawlins, and Henry Hammer reined up while Peter Stone read from a tattered Bible over the three new graves. If there was eventually to be a town at the Devil's Bowler, it already had a boot hill.

Ned removed his hat and sat quietly on Dancer as the eulogy continued. Finally the man with the Bible finished up and turned away. The miners began slowly filling in the open grave.

The well-dressed man, who had started directing the workers, stepped forward as Cody and Hammer approached. Cody realized this must be Polecat Pete. After introducing himself, Hammer, and Rosco, Ned pulled Peter Stone aside to talk. Peter related everything he knew about Saragosa and the mountain, including his story of finding the mine and bringing supplies to the Indian for years. Peter Stone left out one item — the box of Henry shells every month. Some whites looked on providing Indians with firearms or whiskey as a capital crime. He did tell Cody about hiring the Scroggins boys to protect his mining company.

"And he has the woman, Sarah McKinnes, with him," Peter Stone said grimly, concluding his long story. "But I doubt she's fared any better than Frenchy LeConte." A faraway look came into his eye. Then he shook his head sadly and continued. "I've poked around in those caves a little, Sheriff. Unless you've got good lanterns and a lot of men, I'd stay out of there."

"We've got miner's lanterns," Ned replied. "And it's my hope that each of those dogs is worth ten men . . . for tracking, at least."

"Dogs?" Stone asked, puzzled. Rosco had kept the dogs well away from the large group of men.

"We've got three hunting dogs the owner claims will track anything or anyone," Ned said.

Peter Stone shook his head slowly. "I wish you luck," he said. "But I don't envy you. The Scroggins boys took off after the Indian right after he flung Frenchy off the mountain. If you're going on in there, watch out for them."

"We'll be watching out for everything, Mr. Stone," Ned replied grimly. "Obliged for your help."

Ned and Henry walked to where Rosco had tied the dogs, and the three of them gazed up at the ominous mountain.

"I'd give him about a five mile head start," Ned said, "if he wanted to head out of there an' into the desert."

Henry's features hardened. "When we was with the Eleventh Calvary, we run a bunch of Sioux all the way south into Utah and they holed up in a cave. Took us three days to ferret 'em out, and cost four good men. But he had lots of timber and kept fires burning. We finally smoked 'em out. Caught most of 'em, including the leaders. It was no church social, but we got 'em and we'll get this one, particularly with those dogs."

"Well, hell." Ned sighed deeply. "We're not getting' it done standin' here jawin'."

They began loading up with rope, lanterns, and firearms. Then they set out on foot for the entrance from which Ned, Cuen and Ratzlaff had escaped.

Getting into the mountain would be easy, getting out might be another thing all together.

CHAPTER TWENTY-THREE

Sarah McKinnes sat shivering near a smoldering cooking fire in the large cave, her eyes deep set and blank.

Mangas padded softly into the cave, and began loading his pockets with dried meat and mesquite flour. After stuffing his pockets with all the .44/.40 shells he'd gotten from Frenchy and King Hansen, he picked up a rifle and loaded it. He pulled Sarah to her feet and led her, stumbling, to where he had tied the mustang and Two's Riding's pinto. Just as he was about to hoist her into the carved wooden saddle, he stopped. Faintly, he could hear the sounds of approaching footfalls.

Dragging Sarah to the far side of the cave near one of the exit tunnels, Saragosa watched coldly as two bearded men slipped into the cavern. The light from their torches flickered as they moved quickly and silently from stalagmite to stalagmite, never exposing themselves for more than a second.

These men move like Indians, Saragosa thought. Like hunters. All he wanted now was to slip back to the oasis canyon and drive the mules out. He dragged Sarah, still vacant-eyed, into the tunnel. The crack and flash of rifle fire reverberated through the passage. Flying rock chips stung Saragosa's face.

"Thar he is," Shank Scroggins shouted.

Waving at his brother to take the far side of the cavern, they moved rapidly from stalagmite to column, careful never to expose themselves.

Mangas moved deeper into the tunnel, severely hampered by the limp woman he was dragging behind. He grabbed an unlighted torch, carrying it and the rifle in one hand, while pulling Sarah with the other. Returning the rifle fire might help point the way to the tunnel that led outside to the mules. The pursuers could fire at him at their leisure as he rounded up the animals. Besides, the mustang he left in the main cavern was his favorite horse, and he wanted it along on the trip to Colorado. It was important to lead the hunters deeper into the mountain. He didn't need the torch lit. Saragosa knew where he was going in the darkness. But the woman would need it later.

Reaching the tunnel through which the Indian had fled, Shank Scroggins hesitated as he peered into the darkness. He removed the lantern that hung from his belt and lit it. He and Buffalo had extinguished them when Buffalo smelled smoke wafting down the shaft. They had followed the smoke to the main cavern.

The lanterns flared anew, lighting their path. They moved carefully, their backs to the tunnel wall, into the narrow passageway.

Mangas walked swiftly, the woman stumbling along behind. They were moving uphill toward the center of the mountain. The temperature, normally cool in the depths of the mountain, got warmer as they headed upward. Soon the perspiration was dripping from both of them. Sarah followed meekly, completely resigned to whatever fate the Indian had in store for her. The heat, and rotten egg-smelling fumes, began to make her eyes water.

Mangas stopped, knelt, and took his flint and steel from his medicine bag. He frayed some mesquite with his knife, then struck flint to steel and got the torch roaring.

The narrow tunnel widened in front of them. The floor was made up of a series of bubbling, yellow pools. Sour fumes wafted up. They moved forward, treading carefully, never knowing if the patches of yellow mud covering the floor were slime, or the surface of a deep, hellishly hot cauldron.

It was a holy place to Mangas, but he sensed the men who followed would not think so.

Mangas, dragging the girl, deftly negotiated his way around the pools and into a crevice twenty yards beyond. The tunnel narrowed once again. Mangas shoved Sarah deep into a side crevice, pushed her to the floor, and extinguished the torch. Sarah began to moan in the darkness. Mangas reached down and roughly covered her mouth with his hand. But each time he removed it, she began moaning again. He slapped her across the face savagely. She fell silent.

Like a cat, Saragosa padded quietly to the entrance of the tunnel, and stared across the pools of yellow, bubbling mud. Patiently, he waited.

The flashing of lanterns played along the sidewalls. The quiet shuffling of two sets of boots could be heard over the bubbling pools.

"Damn," Shank said, speaking for the first time since they had left the main cavern, "if this ain't a stinkin' mess!" Carefully he lifted the lantern, searching the tunnel on the other side of the room for any sign of the Indian.

Mangas half-closed his eyes, and remained unmoving. He kept his rifle at his side so it wouldn't catch any of the lantern's glow.

His back to the tunnel wall, Shank worked his way slowly around the pools. Buffalo's eyes widened with fear. Buffalo would willingly face a bear and not think twice about it. But he couldn't swim. Suddenly his foot slid out from under him. He grappled at the wall for a hold, dropping his lantern in the process. It slid four feet toward the center of the wide room, then slowly disappeared into the bubbling muck. The mud glowed eerily for a moment then returned to its normal shade as the lamp went out.

"You're as dumb as a pile of buffalo chips," he brother hissed. "Now we only got one lantern."

Shank extended the barrel of his rifle out to the petrified Scroggins. "Hang onto this," he whispered, "and come on." Buffalo shoved his own rifle through his belt, looked uneasily at his brother then complied.

With one hand grasping at a crack in the wall, and one hanging onto his brother's rifle barrel, Buffalo made his way, slowly, gasping, past the last bubbling pool.

"You okay?" Shank asked disgustedly.

"I'm fi—" The roar of a rifle blast made Shank jump as the impact of the shell knocked Buffalo backward. The blood-red splotch on Buffalo's chest widened as he fell to his belly. Clawing desperately, he went sliding downward toward the center of the largest of the mud pools.

Mangas levered in another shell. Shank dropped the lantern and dove to the side behind some mottled yellow boulders. Flame spit from the barrel of Shank's rifle as he returned the fire. But he was shooting into the darkness, seeing no target. Quickly he levered in another cartridge and again fired blindly into the dark tunnel. Other than the sound of the bubbling mud, the tunnel was silent. The last lantern lay in the middle of the tunnel, secure in a shallow hollow. It eerily cast shadows as Shank's eyes searched frantically for his brother. He spotted Buffalo, chest deep in the yellow, grasping mud. Buffalo moaned in terror, slipping in deeper, until the mud had reached his shoulders. Blood bubbled from his mouth in a foamy forth as he slid under. One hand extended from the mud, grasping hopelessly at the air. Then it, too, slipped below the surface. There were a few erratic bubbles. A spot of yellow mud turned orange with Buffalo's blood. Then there was nothing.

"You red bastard!" Shank screamed. "I'm gonna rip your arms off and shove 'em up your butt!"

Saragosa didn't answer. Taking aim at the lantern, still sitting in the middle of the narrowing tunnel, he fired, blowing it apart. The sudden blackness sent a chill up Shank's broad back.

Mangas pulled his knife, determined to dispose of the big man in the darkness. Then he heard the dogs, their yipping and howls echoing from far away down the tunnel.

They heard the muffled sound of shots.

"At least," Henry said, "We know he's up there. And not too far by the sound."

Ned, Henry, and Rosco stood in the middle of the main cavern, flashing their lanterns about. They found the remnants of bandages covered with blood and yellow mud, which Rosco used to scent the dogs. He kept the two females on a ten foot tether, but let the male run free. The animals immediately began ranging around the floor until the male returned to the main cavern. He put his muzzle to the ground and let out the "yip yip" howl that told his master he was on the scent. The broad-chested hound disappeared up a narrow passageway, and the others dragged the little hunter quickly behind.

"Well, it's the fox and the hounds," Ned remarked. "Only this fox has a Winchester."

"I always figured," Henry said, puffing as he ran alongside Ned, "that a man I was chasing . . . was armed to the teeth . . . Unless I saw him standing in the buff . . . Even then I was careful."

They caught up with Rosco. The wiry little man removed a hunter's horn which had been fashioned from the horn of a bull from his belt and blew on it loudly. The sound of the dogs, and the horn, reverberated through the narrow cavern as the man trotted uphill. Rosco stopped. "Damn that hound!" he exclaimed bitterly. "He always gets way out ahead. I don't know how the hell he can see in here. It's blacker than pitch."

They stopped for a moment and listened.

The faraway baying of the male hound and the tugging females spurred them forward. The lantern light flickered off the side walls, ceiling and floors, dancing eerily as the men hurried on. They pulled up short once again, as Ned and Henry caught up with Rosco and the females.

"Is it getting warmer," Henry gasped, "or is it just the running?"

"I think it is getting hotter," Ned said, breathing heavily. "And I smell sulfur."

"We ain't gonna catch him by jawin'," Rosco insisted, not even breathing hard. He trotted away behind the dogs.

"I think," Henry said panting as he ran along behind Ned, "that I'll trade Rosco places . . . and let . . . those dogs . . . pull me. Man was made to sit a saddle . . . not to go by shanks mare!"

Mangas reached deep into the crevice and grabbed Sarah by the wrist. Again he began pulling her up the passageway. He heard the buckskin clad man screaming curses behind him. But Saragosa knew the man would be unable to follow in the dark. There were several different branches of the tunnel. Some of them led to dead ends. Some rose so steeply that a man would have to climb the walls to continue on. Some led to abrupt drop-offs from which Mangas had tossed rocks and never heard them hit bottom. A man would have to be a god to successfully follow Mangas through his mountain. But dogs were different.

Mangas and Sarah came to a spot where the stream surfaced. Again he lit the torch that he'd carefully kept with him. He dropped to his stomach and drank deeply. Sarah filled her hands, and brought them to her mouth several times. But then she retched, puking the water out immediately. When the heaving stopped, she sat back and shivered.

Minutes later they were wading up the stream. After a few yards, it disappeared into a rock face. Mangas began to climb. Sarah attempted to follow, but slipped back. Mangas returned and tried to help her by pushing her up ahead. But her hands would not hold and again she fell, sitting heavily in the stream. Saragosa eyed her coldly. If she could not climb, she could not go with him. Her eyes stared blankly straight ahead. She had the look of a ghost woman in the flickering torch light. Shoving the torch into a crack in the wall, Saragosa began to climb. Alone.

CHAPTER TWENTY-FOUR

Shank Scroggins eased his way along the pitch black tunnel. Then he stopped and stared back down the way he'd come. Dogs. He heard dogs barking. He backed into a crevice and waited.

Shultz, the male hound, ran far ahead of the females and the men. He swerved from one side of the tunnel to the other, sniffing, nose down, then ran straight ahead. Then he stopped. He raised his head, and shook it violently. Something was interfering with the scent, making his eyes water and his nose run.

The lanterns flashed behind him, and soon the female hounds and the men caught up.

"Jesus," Ned gasped when they'd stopped. "I wonder if that smell is poison. The breathin' ain't worth a damn in here."

Rosco reached down and scratched the big dog's ears. "Shultz has lost the scent.

This yellow stuff stinks so bad, he can't track."

Henry was puffing so hard, he couldn't talk. Finally, as they made their way slowly forward, he regained his breath.

"I'll tell you . . . Ned boy," he wheezed, "I'm getting' a little . . . long in the tooth . . . for this sort of thing."

Ned smiled, then yelled to Rosco a few steps ahead. "Rosco, hold up a spell. Let's make damn sure there's no offshoots from this tunnel."

They moved forward slowly. They could just make out the bubbling, steaming, pools of yellow mud. Then they stopped. They jerked their rifles to their shoulders as a man stepped out of the shadows on the other side of the pools.

"I'm sure glad you fellas came along," the stranger said tonelessly, his rifle hanging loosely at his side.

"Scroggins?" Ned asked tentatively.

"Yep." The big bearded man sat down heavily on the slop of the side wall.

"Where's your brother?"

The big hunter looked up. His blank expression turned to one of anger. He pointed to the bubbling pool. "In there," he said bitterly.

None of the men said a word. Finally Ned

spoke up. "Where's the Indian?" he asked.

Scroggins shook his head. "We was on his tail. He went on up this tunnel after he shot out my lantern."

Rosco handed Henry the leashes for the females. Hooking a line onto Shultz, he began to work his way around the pools.

The big dog's feet slipped and slid out from under him. The animal whimpered in terror as Rosco gathered up on the leash to keep him from falling into the bubbling yellow muck. One leg dipped in, and the dog yelped in pain. Rosco worked his way back, and pulled the dog to safety.

"I ain't takin' my dogs this way," he announced. "They done lost the scent anyways. "Let's find another way."

"I'm goin' on," Scroggins insisted. "But I'll need one of those lanterns."

"You hold a minute, Scroggins," Ned replied. He pulled Henry to one side. Keeping his voice low, he asked, "What do you think, Henry?"

The Black man observed the sole surviving Scroggins brother thoughtfully. "Well, that ol' boy looks like he could hunt bear with a switch," he observed. An' I don't guess you give a damn who gets the Indian."

"Just so long as he's got," Ned agreed.

"I say let him have a lantern. Let's work

our way to the top of the mountain. I got a feelin' he's headin' up. I never saw a wild critter that wouldn't, given the chance."

Ned unhooked the lantern from his belt, and walked to the edge of the pools. It was a good twenty feet across. "Can you catch this?" he asked.

"You throw an' I'll catch it," the big hunter replied.

Ned swung the lantern back and forth from its arched wire handle. He lofted it high into the air. Scroggins caught it easily. "I'll be goin' now," he said, and turned to make his way up the tunnel.

It took the rest of them only a few minutes to get back to the main cavern.

"Rosco," Ned said, "I want you to go back to camp. Henry and I'll climb to the top of the mountain. The dogs couldn't get up there anyhow. If the Indian gets off it, we'll use the dogs again."

Rawlins nodded. "Suits me, Cody," he said. He turned and led his animals out the way they'd come.

Ned walked over to the mustang and pinto tethered in the main cavern and slipped their headstalls off. If the Indian returned, his horses would not be where he'd left them. Ned slapped the animals on their rumps and they slowly trotted out ahead.

When they'd reached the mouth of the tunnel, it was dark outside. "Damn! Ned cursed, looking up. "I swore I'd never get on this mountain again in the dark. I swore it fifty times, the last time I climbed it."

"Second time should be easier." Henry said, his tone encouraging.

"Sure it'll be easy, Henry," Ned said, starting the climb. "When pigs can fly."

Mangas had worked his way to the mountain top. As the sun set, he chanted a short prayer to the gods. Then he crossed to the north end of the mountain, where a smooth trough had been formed down the side. It was glass slick. And though it couldn't be climbed, a man could slide down if he was very careful not to go too fast. Saragosa leapt into the trough, careening from one side to the other, using his rifle butt as a brake and rudder as he descended. He slowed, crashed into a gravel flat. Then he stood and worked his way to a cliff side. In the last fading twilight, he could make out the mules grazing in the oasis canyon below.

He could also see the fires of a dozen campsites. Again an internal fire ate at his belly.

Working his way around the mountain, he hesitated at the entrance to the main cavern.

His eyes widened in surprise as he watched the mustang and pinto trotting out. Patiently, he waited. Someone must have turned the horses loose. And that someone would exiting the cave at any moment.

He slunk back into the mesquite rimming the top of the entrance as two men, one black and one white, emerged.

Bringing the rifle to his shoulder, he centered the sight on the white man's back. Deciding there were far too many men camped within earshot, Saragosa lowered his rifle.

The men worked their way along the mountain side away from Mangas. To his surprise, they began to climb. Mangas let them go, then followed the mustang.

Pete sat near the fire, watching the light flicker through the bottle of Napoleon brandy in his hand. It if wasn't for Sarah, he thought, he would have gone on from Mojave and forgotten all about the mine. He had plenty of money. What he wanted was company. Female company. He'd gone far too long without it.

He looked up at the stars, and thought how much nicer it would be if he had someone to enjoy them with. Then the sound of someone approaching made him look up.

He rose, and stared into the darkness. Shank Scroggins stepped into the firelight, with Sarah stumbling behind him.

"Sarah, thank God." Pete rushed forward and took her in his arms. She stood slack, staring at him through deep, vacant eyes.

He stepped back and studied her intently. "Sarah, Sarah. It's me." He took her by the shoulders and shook her gently. "It's Pete," he said, his voice cracking in desperation. "Peter Stone. Polecat Pete!"

Still she said nothing. Pete turned to Scroggins. "Where'd you find her?" he asked.

"Deep in the cave," Scroggins snorted. "Now where's my money?"

"I've got your money," Pete said sitting Sarah carefully on a rock near the fire. She stared into the flame, then lay down on the ground and curled up into a fetal position. Pete turned and exited into his tent.

Moments later he reemerged, holding a pouch of gold dust. He handed the pouch to the bearded hunter who took it and nodded. "I'll be having a bowl of beans, then I'm riding out," Scroggins told him.

"Where's your brother?" Pete asked. "And how 'bout the Indian?"

Scroggins's features darkened. "My brother's dead," he said bitterly, "and the sheriff is chasing the Indian. This is enough money for me."

Scroggins went to the table and grabbed a bowl. Without a word he filled it from the pot of beans that was kept simmering on the fire at all times.

Pete sat down next to Sarah. He took one of her hands in his, but could think of nothing to say. He sat silently staring into the fire.

Mangas watched from the Cliffside near where the mules grazed. The woman lay on the ground near the fire in the miner's camp. The gods were favoring him again. They were returning the woman once more. It was a good omen.

Mangas climbed down and saddled one of the mules. Whipping her up, he started forward, driving the rest of the stock in front of him. He drove them right into the mesquite gate, crashing through it heading straight toward the center of the camp.

Hearing the commotion, Sarah looked up. She turned to a stunned Peter Stone. "Help me, Pete!" she pleaded. "Help me! He's coming again!" The prospector leapt to his feet and stared toward the thundering in the desert. He spun around and started for the tent and his rifle. Then he stopped, realizing the mules would reach the camp before he could return. He ran back toward Sarah, who hadn't moved.

Shank Scroggins looked up from the bowl of beans when he heard the approaching hoof beats. He'd left his rifle leaning against a rock, and now scrambled for it. Pete barreled toward Sarah, yelling, "Sarah, run for the brush! Hurry!" She sat staring, dazed and confused. Pete tried to drag her to her feet, but she was slack and unmovable. At the last moment, Pete dove for the nearby brush.

Shank frantically scanned the approaching mules for a target, but could see nothing. The animals crashed into camp, knocking tables and chairs over, kicking up tent stakes. Shank sank behind a mesquite bush, still searching for a rider.

A big bay mule clattered into view. Before Shank could respond, the Indian, hanging low off the animal's back, fired from beneath her neck. The slug slammed into Shank's chest, driving him back into the mesquite. He clawed at the leather poke that hung from his belt. Satisfied it was safe, the big man died.

Mangas reined the mule around, leaned from the saddle and caught Sarah under the arms in one fluid motion. With a power-ful heave, he lifted her across the saddle in front of him and spurred the animal off behind the others.

Pete leapt from the bush and ran to his fallen tent for his own rifle. But by the time he found it, the hoof beats had faded into the desert.

It had all happened so fast. He'd had Sarah, then lost her again. Men from nearby camps arrived. One picked up a chair and helped Pete into it. Another picked up the bottle of brandy from beside the fire and handed it to him. Pete shakily took a deep draw.

It just wasn't meant to be, he thought, as the burning liquor slid down his throat. It just wasn't meant to be.

Ned and Henry were high on the cliff above oasis canyon when the heard the sound of the mule's hoofs splashing through the creek, then clattering into the desert.

"Damn!" Ned exclaimed, hanging precari-ously from the cliff edge. "You don't sup-pose . . . ?"

"I do suppose," Henry answered. "The Indian must not have gone up. I'd bet a month's pay that it's him pushing those mules out."

"Let's get on down there!" Ned shouted as he began his arduous climb back down. Henry sighed deeply and followed close behind.

Twenty minutes later, Ned was back at the camp. Pete sat with his head hanging between his legs, holding his face in his hands. The other men were out in the brush shouting, calling for Sarah.

"What happened, Mr. Stone?" Ned asked sharply.

Pete shook his head. "That Indian," he croaked. "He rode right into camp, took the woman, an' rode out."

"Woman?" Ned asked.

"Shank Scroggins showed up here with Sarah. But she weren't in camp fifteen minutes before that demon had her again."

Ned hesitated for only a moment then took off with Henry close on his heels. Pete Stone jumped to his feet and yelled after them, "Cody, wait! I'm going too!"

Ned stopped and shouted over his shoulder. "You get back to Mojave and send word to Cuen and Ratzlaff. I want every deputy we've got here as soon as possible. Have Perry call the Army. Both Fort Independence and Fort Mojave. Don't wait, Stone! Ride out now!" The Indian was out of his cave and in the desert again. They were on even ground now, and Ned was ready to take advantage of the situation. It was time for all this to end.

Five minutes later, Ned and Henry were in the saddle again. They would have been even sooner but Henry made Ned slow down and collect what they would need for a long trek into the desert.

As Ned and Henry galloped out, Rosco called after them, "I'll follow as fast as the dogs can travel."

As they sped away, Henry shouted over the clattering hoofs, "Now he's horseback and that's my meat, Cody." Henry charged forward. The tracking was easy in the bright starlight, even though a sliver of a moon was all that shone down at them from the night sky.

Ned set his jaw firmly and concentrated on the trail. Dancer seemed to sense his determination, and raced forward, fighting to pass Henry's buckskin, already pulling far ahead.

CHAPTER TWENTY-FIVE

Mangas rode with the girl laid across the saddle in front of him for a few minutes. Then he reined up, dismounted and pulled her down.

She tried to pull away, but Mangas threw her to the ground and bound her wrists. Then he hoisted her into the saddle of the pinto, tying her hands to the pommel and her ankles to the stirrups. He mounted his own horse and led her off at a canter, pushing the mules ahead.

Sarah began to sob.

Mangas kept up a steady, grueling pace.

The Funeral Mountains ahead were as dry and foreboding as the Panamints, and even further from civilization. When he finally crossed them, he would be in the Colorado desert, and soon, at the Colorado River. Once there, no one would be able to find him, unless he wanted to be found. He would sell the mules, buy enough cartridges to last him for years, and then disappear into the desert. If there were too many men at his sacred mountain to confront head on, he would come at night to kill them. They would leave if he killed enough of them. He could live in the desert as long as he liked. He would have everything he needed — including a woman.

He looked back at Sarah. She stared at him without blinking and without looking away. She was no longer crying. It was good. She was a woman who would bring him good luck. Maybe even sons.

After several hours of riding, Mangas found his way to the east mouth of a deep canyon. Though there was fresh water, it was not a place he particularly wanted to be. Beyond the water hole, the canyon rose too steeply for the mules and horses to climb. Mangas would have to backtrack. But it was the only water for miles plentiful enough to handle all the stock.

The sun was high by the time he reached the water hole. He dragged Sarah from the saddle, hobbled her ankles, but untied her wrists. She fell onto her stomach and drank next to the mules. Then she hopped to a boulder and sat, saying nothing. She was already beginning to burn in the desert sun. But she didn't seem to care.

Mangas retied Sarah's wrists and tied her to the base of a mesquite bush. "Rest," he told her. She looked up at him curiously. At least she would have a little shade. Saragosa led the pinto and the mustang back down the canyon a hundred paces. He tied them securely and climbed high up on the canyon wall to watch his back trail. He sat down and dug the last two pods of peyote out of his medicine bag. Chewing them slowly, he resumed his observation of the desert. His jaw tightened when he saw the unmistakable dust of riders crossing the plain. The woman and the mules would have to wait. He would not be able to get away from the water hole without meeting the riders head on. So they would have to die. He watched until he could make out two riders. Then he returned to the horses and rode back to the water hole.

He dug into a sack he'd tied behind the saddle of the mustang and removed his last half-box of shells. Carrying both .44/.40's, he ran back down the canyon and began to climb the south wall. He wanted the sun at his back when he confronted his enemies.

Henry Hammer reined up, pulled the canteen from his saddle bag, and drank deeply. Ned followed suit. Then they both sat quietly, looking into the red rocks of the deep canyon before them.

"Unless I miss my guess," Henry said, almost as much to himself as to Ned, "that Indian is lookin' to water the stock." They hadn't spoken in six hours of hard riding. Hammer pointed. "See the game trails up high on the canyon walls? They all stay level or head down. Those are desert bighorn trails. They got to get to water every three days or so, and it's my guess there's a big water hole up there." Henry shaded his eyes and searched the horizon of the mountains behind the canyon. "Don't look to me like there's much of anything leading out of the backside of this ol' red rock hole." He turned to stare directly at his friend. "Maybe we found ourselves an Indian trap here, Ned boy."

"Well, let's get on up there before that bastard has a chance to kill that woman. There's been enough killing already." Ned's eyes were cold and hard.

Hammer put his hand on Cody's shoulder. "Let's not rush it, Ned. He didn't bring her along just to kill her. He could've done that plenty of times. If he's up there, he'll be watchin' us right now. Dismount, cause we're walking from here on."

Ned shook Hammer's hand off violently.

"I'm sick of this, Henry," he said. "Let's charge in there and get this bastard."

Henry frowned. "I for one don't want to go home feet first," he admonished his friend. He's sitting up in those rocks waitin' for some dumb pilgrim to play it just like you're suggesting. You charge in there and, friend or not, you're charging in alone."

Ned sighed and dismounted.

They started the long walk into the canyon.

Mangas climbed until he reached a spot where he could see far down into the canyon. He was a mile from the mouth, and couldn't see the floor immediately below, but could see out toward the mouth for a good way.

He waited patiently, not even moving to shoo away the flies buzzing about his eyes.

Henry had positioned himself and Cody between the horses in the narrow canyon bottom. They moved forward at a steady pace. He looked over at Ned, who searched the canyon floor in front of them. "The horses will sense him if he's down in the bottom, Ned," Henry advised. "Just watch the canyon sides and the skyline. If he's the shot you say he is, he'll be up there waitin'."

"Or ridin' the hell away with the woman,"

Ned replied grumpily.

"Maybe, maybe no. But —" Before he could finish, Ned dove into him, knocking the black man sprawling to the ground. A rifle shot slammed into the buckskin with a splat, before the sound of the shot echoed throughout the canyon. Ned, dragging Dancer, ran to the south wall.

"I saw the flame from the muzzle," he explained breathlessly as he and Henry crowded against the steep canyon wall.

The buckskin reared, let out a pitiful scream, and began to gallop out of the canyon. He ran twenty yards, then stumbled, going rear end over fore-shoulders. He tired to rise, blowing bloody froth from his muzzle and nose, but fell to his side. His chest heaved, and he kicked in a vain effort to get to his feet. Henry brought his rifle to his shoulder and shot the buckskin in the head. The horse was suddenly stilled.

"That son-of-a-bitch," Henry muttered angrily. "That was the finest ropin' horse a man ever rode. An' he pulled me outta more'n one blizzard."

"Now what?" Ned asked, his voice hushed.

The older man grunted. "At least we know where he is." Henry surveyed the canyon above him. "Ned, you mount up. This time it's hell for leather. As soon as you get out of the cover of the wall, drop as low as you can on the left side of your animal. I'm gonna sashay up this wall and try to get a shot at him while he's concentrating on you."

"When?"

"Give me to the count of twenty-five . . . a slow count."

"One," Ned began as Henry began climbing.

Sarah flinched when she heard the gunshots. She sat up, noticing with surprise that she was no longer sweating and shivering. And for the first time in days she was hungry.

"Twenty-five," Ned counted.

He swung up into the saddle and spurred the big horse on. Dancer flung gravel out behind him like bullets as he drove his body forward with his powerful hindquarters.

Mangas had been concentrating on the skyline near where he had seen the men take cover. He figured the men would try to climb up to get a shot at him. They could not possibly leave. Two white eyes with one horse would never make it across the desert.

Saragosa heard the clattering of the horse's hoofs seconds before he saw it break from the cover of the overhang. The Indian raised the .44/.40 quickly to his shoulder. As he drew a bead on the rider, the man dropped to the far side of the horse. Before Mangas could lower the muzzle to the chest of the horse, both the mount and its rider disappeared behind the canyon wall.

A slug sang off the rock wall directly behind Mangas, stinging him with splinters of rock. The Indian dove to the other side of the boulder. His eyes searched the skyline.

He saw movement. The top of a hat appeared over the ledge. Instantly Saragosa had the rifle lined up on the target. He squeezed off a shot and the hat flew away. Immediately the Indian knew he'd been tricked. The hat had been placed atop a stick. As Mangas was levering in another shell, a black man jumped up a few feet away from where the hat had been. The man quickly snapped off another shot. For the second time a slug slammed into the canyon wall behind Mangas. He leapt up and fired. The rock in front of the now hatless Hammer sprayed rock chips around as the ricochet whined away.

Mangas scrambled around a rock ledge, and up the canyon on a narrow game trail, carrying two rifles. He levered the shells out of one, and propped it up in the rocks. Its barrel stuck out in plain view. Then Saragosa ran thirty yards further up the trail and dropped behind another rock ledge.

Cody drew rein. Before Dancer slid to a full stop, Ned was already on the ground and running. He found Sarah McKinnes sitting on the ground, tied to the base of a mesquite. He palmed his knife and cut her free. She barely acknowledged his presence. He ran back down the canyon and began climbing its south face.

Henry peered over a ledge. He could see the protruding barrel of the rifle. But it didn't move, nor did he see anyone behind it, so he was wary. It was too steep to climb up, so Henry dropped twenty feet down the slope. He eyed the rifle barrel, but also visually searched every nearby hiding place. It wouldn't be the first time an Indian had abandoned his rifle in favor of his knife. Perhaps the man was out of shells.

Looking up, Henry spotted a covey of quail flushed out farther up the trail. It was either the Indian, or Ned returning.

Rounding a turn in the game trail, Ned saw motion in the distance. In addition to his .44./.40, Ned was wearing his converted

Dragoon Colt. The shots had worried him. Cody had the rifle to his shoulder before he realized his intended target was Henry. Ned let his rifle fall.

Since one man had passed him on the floor of the canyon and one was behind him, Mangas knew that he was hemmed in. The man behind was apparently not falling for the rifle in the rocks trick. With no other options, he jumped into the ravine that went all the way to the bottom of the canyon. Saragosa slid quickly not using his rifle for a brake or rudder.

As Cody stepped around the turn in the trail, he saw the Indian gathering speed in the ravine bottom. Before he could snap off a shot, the Indian fired.

The slug slammed into Cody's side, spinning him around. He too began a rapid slide down the face of the steep mountain.

Henry Hammer stepped into view just as Mangas fired at Cody. Hammer snapped off a shot, levered in and fired again. He fired a third time as the Indian went sliding into the ravine.

Tumbling down the sandstone slope, alongside the Indian, Ned tried desperately to hang onto the rifle. But despite his efforts, it clattered away. Cody managed to palm the Colt as he slid to a near stop on the steep cliff side. He snapped off a shot as the Indian tumbled by. Ned began sliding again, but was able to fire twice more at the Indian. Ned crashed heavily into a boulder, spun away, and slid again. He rolled to a stop, nearly unconscious. He breathed deeply several times, and his vision finally cleared. Ned struggled to his feet, grasping at his side, trying to stem the bleeding from his wound. The blood gushed between his fingers.

He heard a cry like that of an eagle, and looked up. The massive Indian was limping toward him, the blood flowing freely from a red, meaty hole in his leg. Saragosa stopped and raised his rifle.

Ned raised the Colt in a fluid motion and fired. The slug hit the Indian high on the right chest, spinning him around and driving him backward. Saragosa dropped the rifle and fell to one knee.

Ned fired again. This time he gut-shot the Indian as he moved forward toward his rifle. Ned steadied himself, and fired once more as the Indian rose up. Another slug hit the Indian in the middle of the chest. Mangas staggered backward. Ned knew he was finished. But, almost impossibly, Saragosa steadied himself and headed for his rifle.

More than a man, Ned thought as he sank to one knee. Saragosa collapsed to both of his, just managing to reach out and grasp his rifle. He raised the muzzle.

Ned fought to stay conscious as he cocked the .44 Colt. The Indian slowly, deliberately, levered in another shell, the blood now flowing freely from his mouth and nose.

Ned centered the Colt on the Indian's forehead, and pulled the trigger. The sickening click of the hammer on the empty chamber echoed through the canyon. Ned's vision began to blur out as he saw the octagonal barrel of the Indian's .44/.40 center on his own forehead.

Through a haze, Cody heard the growl of an angry animal, followed by the roar of a muzzle blast that was so loud it deafened for a moment. The sheriff fell forward, his face in the sand of the canyon bottom. Then everything went black.

CHAPTER TWENTY-SIX

When Ned came to, Al Cuen was standing over him, his still-smoking shotgun in his hand. Rosco's big dog, Shultz, was busily licking Cody's face.

Ned tried to sit up, but Cuen pushed him back down. "Where the hell did you come from?" Ned managed to get out.

"I started back for Mojave as soon as I got your telegram," Cuen explained. "It doesn't take both Ratzlaff and myself to watch over the town. And besides," Cuen grinned. "That big Indian cut my reata in half. My father gave me that reata. I wasn't going to let you go after him alone. I caught up with Rosco Rawlins and Peter Stone out on the desert. One of the dogs was sore footed. Stone, Shultz here and I came on ahead. Rosco will be along any time."

Henry Hammer rounded a turn in the canyon bottom, puffing and gasping. Seeing Al, he raised the rifle.

"Hold on, Henry," Cody yelled. "He's a deputy!" Henry lowered the rifle and walked to where the Indian lay. The blast from Al's shotgun had taken him in the middle of the chest and a well-placed shot from Peter Stone's .44/.40 had put a perfect hole in his forehead. Plus the Mojave's throat was ravaged where the big dog had leapt at him.

"That was about," Ned muttered, "the meanest son-of-a-bitch I've come across since Preacher Gatlin was my straw boss. Help me up, Al." Ned reached for his friend and attempted to rise.

Al helped Ned to his feet. Together they stumbled back up the canyon. Ned gritted his teeth, saying nothing. It was forty yards to the mules and the water hole.

Ned leaned on Al's shotgun, and looked at the two people standing near the water hole. Sarah McKinnes and Peter Stone stood, looking into each other's eyes. But Sarah still had the blank look of non-recognition.

Henry made Ned lie down and investigated the wound in his side. Luckily the bullet had passed through cleanly. "Damn," Henry complained, "hoped I'd get to show you how sharp my skinning knife is."

They found shelter under an overhang near the water hole, and erected a semipermanent camp.

As the shadows reached across the canyon bottom, Cuen, Rosco, and Henry Hammer walked the few yards down the canyon to where Mangas Saragosa lay sprawled in the ravine bottom. Rosco had left Shultz tied nearby to keep the predators away from the Indian.

As they approached, one lone ray of sunlight found its way to the canyon floor, casting its glow on the prostrate body of the massive Indian. Even in death, he looked formidable.

"We're going to have to be here awhile," Cuen said. "With this heat, we can't take him back. I guess we'd better bury him."

It was almost sundown by the time they finished the job. As they walked back to the water hole, the dogs answered the call of the coyotes, the echoes bouncing off the walls of the canyon.

A lone eagle dipped down from the sky, so close that Cody could hear the swish of his wings as he passed only twenty feet above. Seeing the men and the dogs, it screamed in annoyance, caught an updraft, and soared high above the canyon's edge. The last rays of the sun flashed golden on his wings. And then he was gone.

■ ■ ■ ■

For three days, while Ned Cody healed, Peter Stone sat by the fire and held Sarah's hands. He combed her long sable hair, comforting her with soft words. Most of the time she stared blankly into the fire. But she was eating the soup Peter fixed and fed to her.

She was not the Sarah McKinnes Peter Stone had offered the reward for oh so long ago. She was blank and slack, almost inanimate — not pretty and certainly not lively.

She ate when food was offered, went to the crude privy Peter had built especially for her, and slept. But she never spoke, nor smiled.

Peter Stone, who'd finally found a woman he thought could replace the one he'd lost so long ago, had lost this one much more quickly. Polecat Pete, who'd cleaned up for a woman, now, ironically, had a woman with no interest in cleaning herself.

Finally, Ned announced he was fit to ride. Al Cuen helped him into the saddle. When Pete led Sarah's horse over, ready to help her into the saddle, something miraculous happened. She smiled, weakly, to be sure, but a smile nonetheless. She said hoarsely

"Thank you," and reached out to lay a hand alongside Pete's cheek. "Thank you for everything."

Pete reached out and took her joyfully in his arms. She dropped her head to his shoulder and began to weep quietly. He looked at the other men with tears in his eyes. "Y'know," he said, his voice cracking, "that's the first time she's done anything 'sides rockin' or moanin' since she come out a' that mountain."

"It's been bottled up inside her," Ned said, smiling. Then Pete, too, began to weep.

"If that ain't the damndest thing," Henry Hammer mumbled, shaking his head. Al Cuen finished saddling his horse, then reached into the saddlebag and fished out a bottle of *aguardiente*.

"Speakin' of bottles, Henry," he said, pulling the cork. "What say we all cry over this until the rest of these folks are ready to ride."

"Yes, sir, Mr. Cuen," Henry said, reaching for the bottle. "That's what I call somethin' to whine about."

Ned dismounted and dropped Dancer's reins. He walked over and took the offered bottle from Henry. "I might as well join in," he grumbled. "Yesterday was Mary Beth's birthday, and I got a feeling she celebrated it by announcing her unengagement."

"Then we must drink the whole bottle," Cuen said cheerfully. "Ned just got a pardon."

Henry and Al laughed loudly. But Ned didn't crack a smile as he took a long draw. Over on the side, oblivious to the others, Sarah was telling Pete how much she wanted to see San Francisco.

Alvarado Cuen began to hum a Mexican melody.

An eagle screeched in the distance.

ABOUT THE AUTHOR

L. J. Martin is the author of more than 45 book-length works (westerns, historicals, mysteries, thrillers, and non-fiction), and has written a number of screenplays, two of which have been optioned. L. J. has written a number of series, both western and crime. His non-fiction books include: *Killing Cancer* (he's a two time cancer survivor); *Write Compelling Fiction*, an instructional work for aspiring authors; *Myrtle Mae & the Crew*, a book of cartoons; *From the Pea Patch*, a conservative political series of essays; *Cooking Wild & Wonderful*, a cookbook with story content; *The California Cocina*, a historical cookbook; *Building a Greenhouse*, a how-to book.

L. J. and his wife Kat Martin, a *New York Times* bestselling, internationally published romantic suspense and historical romance author, live in Montana in the Spring, Summer, and Fall and on the California coast in the Winter.

When not writing, L. J. is cooking and developing recipes for his website The Kitchen at Wolpack Ranch (www.wolfpack ranch.com); hunting, fishing, or hauling his cameras around the high country; or promoting his and Kat's careers. He has two dozen novels and non-fiction works listed on Amazon and Kindle.

The employees of Thorndike Press hope you have enjoyed this Large Print book. All our Thorndike, Wheeler, and Kennebec Large Print titles are designed for easy reading, and all our books are made to last. Other Thorndike Press Large Print books are available at your library, through selected bookstores, or directly from us.

For information about titles, please call:
  (800) 223-1244

or visit our website at:
  gale.com/thorndike

To share your comments, please write:
  Publisher
  Thorndike Press
  10 Water St., Suite 310
  Waterville, ME 04901